Dedication

This book is dedicated to the one person that makes my life worth living, my best friend and wife, Karen. For some reason she has chosen to love me despite the me I am and for that I am forever thankful.

Part One-Page Two

Part Two-Page Eighty Nine

CHOOSING

Face the facts of being what you are, for that is what changes what you are. Soren Kierkegaard

PART ONE

CHAPTER ONE

He walked along the hills of Southern Indiana overlooking the Ohio River. Against the path limestone rocks jutted from the earth as if they were part of a fortress against the invading marauders of time bringing the future. It was clear they had lost the countless battles over the years but perhaps in the end victory would be theirs'.

Resting on a rock along the path he watched as the muddy water of the Ohio flowed toward the Mississippi River. In the distance a tiny tug boat struggled against the currents pushing four barges up the Ohio toward Louisville. As the tiny tug boat disappeared around the bend of the river. another tiny tug boat pushed six barges with the current downstream toward Evansville or places unknown.

Resting there he looked at the muddy water and could not help but wonder if the next step he was to take was into the future or the past. As he pondered the next step, the words he had wrote but three weeks earlier haunted him, "In the darkness of the night I looked back at the horizon and my life and saw there a desolate desert that lead to places unknown. Gathering courage I began a journey into the shifting sands that lead from whence I came to where I was going. It was in the long treacherous journey I found the lost soul that was I."

He was Joseph Samuels standing six foot three with wavy brown hair, a narrow face, strong jaw, thin lips, and small dimples when he smiled. His lean muscular body and strong deep brown eyes projected confidence, but it was a deception; beneath the exterior was a shy backward boy living inside the shell of a man. Time had created a man over the frame of a shy uncertain boy.

Joseph grew up the only child of Bertha and William Samuels in the small Southern Indiana town of Arlington. It was a place forgotten by time and the creek that once drew folks to the town. The creek once flowed strong through the valley bringing traders and goods to the town but over time it lost interest in the ways of the past and began to send most of its' heavy waters to more prosperous places. The old Farm Store stood at the center of the town; a tomb in the graveyard of the past that was the town. Once it stood a grand beacon of commerce. Now rotting boards and windows boarded to stop the miscreants from their nightly reigns of terror was all that was left. A sad reminder that time had passed the town by.

There were still a thousand or so folks that called Arlington home. Most drove the six miles to Pelican Point to work at the chair factory.

Why they remained in the town that time had passed was unknown to even them. It was if they grew up and just simply didn't have a better idea so stayed.

Bertha and William fell in love; at least that is what they told Joseph. The truth was they just figured they could not find anybody better around town. So their future as man and wife began as a result of their giving up, it was an Arlington tradition. William often said, "I settled and she figured she couldn't do much worse so she did as well. Now here we are married folks." They both could not imagine moving beyond Arlington into the unknown, so they settled down in a small trailer just across from the railroad tracks. The train didn't bother coming through Arlington these days so they were never bothered by the noise of the engine making its way. Their existence was one of comfort in knowing the world around them.

William Samuels was raised on a farm south of town where he spent his youth working in the fields trying to avoid his Father's cane. His Father, Morton, walked with a limp due to a mule kicking him as a child. However, the cane was more a weapon then a crutch. Morton could often be seen chasing his son through the fields with his cane raised without a limp.

William had six brothers and five sisters in a small four room cabin. No one could ever figure why but William's family was a cast of characters. Lou Martin, the banker, once said, "It's like a Tennessee Williams' play lost its characters on a visit to Arlington."

Lucy Jones, the leader in Arlington society responded with distain, "No, it is like a circus came to town and let the clowns loose."

The Samuel's tended to see life as if it was a giant stage and their goal was to play their role in a way that kept the spotlight on them. As a result they were always doing something that was the talk of the town. William was the black sheep of the family never amounting to much although in the early days he had dreams. He dreamed of being a successful farmer, a banker, a lawyer, or policeman, the problem with his dreams was they required effort on his part he wasn't willing to expend. Of course in his mind his dreams never came to fruition because of some unforeseen force. He often said when he was with bottle, "Those rich folks won't share their wealth. They just want to use it to keep us poor folks down here in the gutter."

He failed to make it to his senior year due to a failing marks and a fight with the math teacher. During the summer before his second time as a junior he was arrested for stealing Mable Elrod rings out of her purse while she was looking at some candy at the drug store. Given his arrest he decided it was time to leave school behind.

Leaving school behind was the end of his dreams; now it was time to find a job. He followed the town tradition and went to Pelican Point to the chair factory and got a job boxing chairs.

Having a job meant he could do what everyone else did in Arlington get married and settle down. So, the only girl he knew well enough to ask to marry was Bertha. So after a few dates he asked her to settle down with him in his trailer on the other side of the tracks. In most places living on the other side of the tracks is a bad thing but in Arlington there was no good side of the tracks.

The work in the factory was hard most days he went home with his shirt soaking wet from the sweat. Every night they sat at the dinner table and eat a fried bologna sandwiches Bertha had fixed with some cold ice tea. Most nights they sat on the two steps to their trailer and watched as people walked by until time for sleep came. The next morning at five they would be up preparing for their day. Bertha worked cleaning houses for a group of ladies that were considered high society in Pelican Point. Going from one house to the next, day after day scrubbing the toilets, ironing clothes, doing dishes that had accumulated and then Bertha would make her way back home and fix dinner. Some days Bertha would try to ease through the day because her back was hurting, but more often than not the lady of the house would suspect she was slacking off and say, "Bertha, I need the house cleaned good. We will have company tomorrow and I don't want them thinking I don't keep a clean house. So, please get to work."

Despite everything Bertha and William were happy with their lives. As William often said to Bertha, "We got each other, a place to live, and food on the table, what else could we want?"

William came home one night and saw on the table a hamburger with fried potatoes. Looking up at Bertha he asked, "Wow what is the occasion?"

Bertha wiped the tears from her eyes as she said, "We are going to have a baby."

William grabbed Bertha and they held each other as the tears of joy fell. Finally, William pulled away, "How far along are you? Are you sure?"

"I am sure. I am three months along."

William went to work the next day on cloud nine telling everyone he passed about the baby. As the day passed the sweat pouring down his face didn't seem to matter as he continued to think of Bertha and the baby and the future. It was late in the day when Warren Moore, owner of the company, stopped to talk to William, "My boy is coming home. He didn't make it in college. He spent too much time partying and not enough studying."

"I'm sorry to hear that," William said curious as to why Mr. Moore was sharing this with him since he had never before stopped to talk to him.

"You know sales have been down for some time now so we haven't been making any money these past three years. I have done my best to keep the doors open but it hasn't been easy."

"We understand sir. That is why no one has been arguing for a raise the last three years." In the back of his mind William thought, 'But you still had enough money to pay for the new Mercedes and keep the pool open.'

"I appreciate that. But the thing is since my boy is coming back I have to find him a job here, I have to let someone go."

William eyes got big since he now knew why Mr. Moore was talking to him, "Yes?"

"If he is going to learn the business he needs to start at the bottom so I am going to have him do the boxing. I hate it but I don't have anything else for you to do here."

William stood there with a stunned look trying to get his mind to comprehend what was happening. Finally he said, "Haven't I done a good job?"

"Yes, but I have to take care of family. Don't make this difficult and I'll give you a good reference."

William said nothing as he just shook his head.

Making his way home William figured he would tell Bertha but as he opened the door she began talking about the possible names for the baby, so he held the news within figuring he would tell the next day after he found another job.

The next morning he left at the regular time but with nowhere to be he just wandered around the streets waiting until some of the businesses were open so he could go in and apply for a job. Each place he said if they were hiring he was the kind of fellow they would hire but they weren't at the moment, so he continued looking. Finally late in the day he went to his Uncle George's place, a little hardware store on the south side of town. George was his Father's brother who made his money in the hardware business. The day they buried William's Father Uncle George took him aside and said, "If you ever need anything just let me know." Now he needed something, he needed a job.

The problem for William was his Uncle George said things he didn't mean when he was drunk. So, when William told him about needing a job Uncle George paused a moment and said, "You wouldn't be out of work if you had done a good job. They don't fire good workers." Compassion was not a part of his makeup.

William was a bit taken aback by his Uncle, "I did a damn good job; he just wanted a place for his son. Look you said if I ever needed anything to let you know. Well I need a job."

"Look boy I ain't no miracle worker. My business is down what with the new Walmart in town. I may not be open in six months if I don't cut my overhead."

"So you got nothing?"

"No, I ain't got a damn thing, sorry."

William looked at his Uncle realizing he was reaching the end of the line and hope was fading, "Thanks for nothing."

Tired frustrated and scared William stopped at the Depot Bar to get a drink. Mickey Sanders from the Chair factory laughed as William sat down, "Hell it took two people to replace you."

William looked at his drink a moment, "What are you talking about?"

"The boss' son got so far behind the first day they had to hire him an assistant."

"What are you talking about?"

"The boy got things in such a mess up there they hired someone to help him."

William held his beer in his hand and finally slammed it down as he walked away, "Damn that son of a bitch."

William hurried down to the factory offices to confront his boss. Walking into the office he found the boss sitting behind a desk reading the paper with a cigar in his mouth.

William walked into the room and asked, "Did you hire someone to help your son pack chairs?"

"Yes, but that is no concern of yours."

"The hell it isn't. You fired me to give him my job. Why didn't you at least let me be the one to help him?"

"Look boy he wanted his friend to work with him, so that is what we did. Now get out of here and quit bothering me."

William walked away angry with himself for not telling his boss what he thought of him. He kept asking himself over and over, 'I must enjoy being a door mat for these people.' Finally he stopped and swore to himself, 'I'm tired of them taking and taking. I am going to start taking. It is time I made this damn life fair.'

As he walked pass his boss' house he saw a pair of hedge clippers that have been left by the scrubs, picking them up he went on down the street. He would come back by his boss' house several times over the next few weeks picking up things that had been left outside. William told himself, 'He owes me. They all owe me.'

Finally, William had to tell Bertha he had lost his job. She looked at him and said, "Dear that is ok, we'll get through this." She believed it but William knew they wouldn't. He knew they would never be the same, he would never be the same person he once was. He was bitter angry and it was slowly taking what she once knew of him leaving a bitter angry man. As his bitterness took control he gave into the bottle to seek escape from the failure he knew he was. Stealing became his way of making money and getting even with the people in the world that owed him.

Sitting alone at home after Bertha had left for work William heard a knock at the door. There at the door was Bernard, his brother. Bernard had once been the Arlington Police Chief until the incident with Doctor Monroe. Bernard was a good Samuels in that he played his part with real gusto always hungry for attention. He talked with a deep southern drawl although he had never ventured further south than Louisville, Kentucky strutting around town in neatly pressed uniform, polished silver platted gun, and a unlighted cigar hanging out of his mouth. As police chief Bernard saw everything as either right or wrong, there was no middle ground. One either obeyed the law or one didn't. It was that philosophy that led to the famous Doctor Monroe incident. The good doctor was driving 45 miles an hour in a 35 mile an hour zone through town one Thursday morning so Bernard put on the siren and took chase. As the doctor stopped he got out of the car and informed Bernard he was in a hurry because Willow Jones had gone into labor and was about to have her baby at home. Bernard seeing no excuse for breaking the law informed the doctor he was going to give him a ticket. The doctor a man of few words responded to the situation, "Look you idiot I have to get going I don't have time to waste on this petty ticket. You can bring it by the office."

As the good doctor began to get back in his car Bernard decided to arrest him for disorderly conduct after all his conduct was not respectable, so he put the cuffs on him and hauled him to jail. That night a special session of the town council ordered Bernard to appear and the town board president informed him, "Bernard we had hoped you would use some commonsense in this job. Luckily Willow's husband delivered the baby, although he was traumatized by the whole thing and has been sitting in a room alone crying ever sense. We are going to let you go."

Bernard walked out of the meeting with his head held high knowing he was on the right side of the law. Since then he had been driving semis for Taylor Trucking; making long haul delivers all over the country.

As William opened the door Bernard stormed in, "You little fool, how you been?"

"I'm fine, what are you doing here?"

"Life couldn't be better. I'm driving through to California and thought I would see if you wanted to get a drink before I headed out. Come on let's go to the Depot and have a few."

"Ok, but I ain't got no money."

"No problem boy, I got us plenty."

William and Bernard sat at the Depot the rest of the day and into the night drinking talking about the good times. It was eight that evening when Bernard turned to William, "Look boy I hate to drive out to California by myself. Why don't you come along."

"I have to find a job. I don't have time to waste."

"Well boy look I will pay you. You can drive some so you will be working for me. What do you say?"

Riding in a truck to California and getting paid sounded like a good deal so he said yes. After a couple more beers they stopped at the trailer to tell Bertha where he was headed. She hated to see him go but if he could make a little money this way then it was best.

As they began to drive out of town William realized Bernard's outlook on the law had changed. There was no longer a right or wrong; it was just whatever you could get by with. So as he pulled the truck onto the highway and grabbed the beer between his legs and took two little pills in one big gulp. William was surprised to see his brother taking medicine so he asked, "Have you been sick?"

"Sick, hell no. These pills are to keep my eyes open. We got a long way to go and I drive better awake then asleep."

Driving through Nebraska Bernard finally turned to William, "Hey it is time for you to drive. I need to do a bit more drinking and get some shut eye."

William got behind the wheel and with a couple spurts began moving forward. Bernard looked over as he opened another beer, "If you see the police pulling you over tell me and I'll get behind the wheel."

"Why?"

"Because you ain't licensed to drive this thing," Bernard said laughing.

They made it to Nevada as William gave up the driving to Bernard. Suddenly Bernard pulled off the interstate and headed north. William looked at the map, "You are headed the wrong way. California is that way."

"Boy, I got to get me some sugar up the road."

It wasn't long until Bernard pulled the truck into a parking lot across from a massage parlor with a huge sign that said, "Full Body massage." Getting out of the truck he turned to William, "You want to get some sugar?"

"No, I'm ok."

"I figured as much you ain't been married long enough to be wantin' sugar. I'll be back in a few."

Thirty minutes later Bernard slide into the truck with a smile on his face, "California here we come."

The problem the closer they got to their destination the drunker Bernard was getting and the more pills he was taking. As they pulled into Cupertino, California Bernard turned to William, "I am going to throw up." Pulling the truck off the road he got out and made his way to the back of the truck and began puking. William walked around back to check on him and said, "Look I got to piss. I am going up there behind those trees."

Standing behind a tree William saw the flashing lights of a police car as it pulled up to Bernard. He heard some yelling and cursing as he ducked behind some bushes and watched as they threw Bernard in the police car and drove off. Standing there in the bushes William wondered, 'What am I going to do. Bernard has the money. I don't have anything.'

He began to push his way through the bushes tearing his shirt on the limbs. He figured there must be a place somewhere down this road he can get some help so he began walking. Walking down the street he saw a repair truck sitting by the street with a shirt hung on the mirror with a tool belt across the hood. Figuring this might be his way to get back home he grabbed the shirt and tool belt and kept walking down the street. He needed a shirt to replace his torn one and the tool belt with tools he could use to pawn someplace. Pulling the shirt on he hurried down the street.

He continued walking thinking he would find a pawn shop but he saw nothing. Finally he saw a building that looked like a manufacturing business. Tired of walking he walked into the front doors in hopes he could get some directions. Walking up to the front desk the young lady looked up with sweat on her forehead, "I thought you weren't coming."

"What?"

"I told your company we couldn't pay what they required. All we can pay is $1,000 in cash and $1,000 worth of shares in the company."

William realized he had the repair company's name on his shirt, "Look lady I am here on my own time. So, I'll do the job for that. What is it you need fixed."

"Great, the air condition of course, like I told them. The system is out back. Please fix it I am burning up. I can't stand this heat," she said wiping the sweat from her brow. "The system is in the back of the building of course, please hurry."

Walking to the back of the building he figured he would stay back there a while work up a sweat and go back in and hopefully she would feel sorry for him and maybe give him a $100 for his time. Seeing the air conditioner unit he decided he would take the outer cover off and see if he could perform a miracle and then he saw the problem. Caught in the fan was a dead rat. Yanking it out suddenly the blades began turning. He had fixed it. Putting the cover back on he sat down figuring he shouldn't go in quite yet, he needed to make it look like he had to spend more time working on the unit. 'This is my lucky day after all,' he thought.

After taking a nap he got to his feet and made his way to the front desk. The young woman had a huge smile on her face, "Oh my that cool air feels so good. Here let me pay you." She reached into her desk and pulled out a thousand dollars and four pieces of paper.

As she handed the paper to William he asked, "What are these?"

"They are the stock certificates I told you we would pay along with the thousand dollars. I need the name to put on them."

William feared getting his name was a trap so they could arrest him; for what he didn't. So he gave them the name of his baby boy back home, Randy.

William smiled took the money and paper and walked out the door. He thought about throwing the paper in the trash but he realized Bertha would find it really funny he got partially paid in paper.

Once he made it home he told her the story of the repair job and pulled out the paper he had received in payment, "Did you ever hear of anyone paying you in paper?"

Bertha laughed, "No dear that is the funniest thing I have ever heard of."

William started to throw the papers in the trash but Bertha stopped him, "I want to keep them. We will tell our friends the story and we will need the proof." Grabbing them she put them in a shoe box she kept under the bed.

CHAPTER TWO

Some people went to work but William went to steal any place he could find something unguarded. Growing up Joseph never felt the need to question his Father when he came home in the evening with some treasure he said he had found. Joseph assumed his Father was just lucky. Over time as he grew older he came to realize his Father wasn't lucky at all, he was a thief.

Joseph and his Mother were the only ones that worked. Joseph spent his summer days working on the Logan farm and evenings working at the Corner Grocery Store. Most nights he finished at ten went home to bed exhausted only to do it all over the next day starting a five. One evening walking in the door he found his parents packing. Looking around as his Mother put the few dishes in a box and his Father hurriedly throwing clothes in a bag he asked, "What is going on?"

"Oh dear, we are moving. I need to be closer to my work at the Childress family house," Bertha said hurrying around the room.

"Yeah boy we got us a trailer in Brighton. Much better place. So hurry and get your things packed," William said motioning to Joseph to hurry.

The truth was the local police chief told William he and the rest of the town were tired of him stealing everything around town and if he didn't get out of town he would put him in jail even if he couldn't prove anything. William decided the chief might be able to prove something so they better be moving.

Moving to Brighton meant Joseph would be going to a different school leaving the few friends he had behind. It was just another ride on the roller coaster that was his life with Bertha and William Samuels. He took a deep breath and packed knowing in the back of his mind something was not being said.

Joseph walked into his new school the first day in the fall and looked around lost. Standing at his locker he watched as everyone passed him as if he were invisible. Standing at his locker he watched as a young man with short blonde hair and a muscular body pushed his way down the hall bumping into the girl at the locker next to Joseph's as he said, "Watch where you are going fatso." He continued pushing his way pass until Joseph reached out and grabbed his arm. "Hey you don't talk that way to her. You should say excuse me."

The blond hair boy looked at Joseph and said, "Do you know who I am?"

"No, I don't know who you are and I don't care. You don't talk to a lady that way."

The blonde hair boy drew his fists up to throw a punch but before he could get his fists above his waist Joseph landed a clean solid hit to his chin. Falling against the lockers he looked up and started to spring to his feet when joseph kicked him in the one place that would get his full attention. As the blonde hair boy cried in pain Joseph leaned forward, "Look, if you ever treat this girl that way again I will remove your testicles one at a time while you watch."

As Joseph looked at the young girl next to him he asked, "Can I walk you to your class? What is your name?"

The young girl with beautiful blue eyes and long blonde hair and a round body said, "I am Missy. Yes you can walk with me. I am going to my Algebra class."

"Great, so am I."

Missy had spent her years in school being laughed at and teased by her classmates, so it was no surprise when the high school quarterback called her names. But then someone came to her defense a person she had never seen before. As Missy sat down in the Algebra class Lisa laughed, "Do you think that chair is strong enough to hold you?" Sitting in the back of the room, Joseph heard Lisa walking up to her, "Look you ugly bitch if you ever say something like that to her again I'll shave you bald."

Bobby sitting next to Lisa said, "You shouldn't talk to her that way." Joseph just looked at him and smiled as he swung his fist hitting Bobby's desk, "I'll say what I want when I want. Don't ever tell me do anything again. You understand?"

The events of the day spread through the school, everyone knew Missy now had a protector and no one knew how far this strange person would go so the teasing ended. Of course Missy was uncertain as to why she had a protector so she asked Joseph, "Why are you doing this?"

"I like you. I don't think anyone should treat you that way. There is no more to it than that."

Missy and Joseph sat every day at lunch by themselves talking about their lives. Missy was the daughter of a well to do farmer who saw her as a failure. Joseph was the son of a failure who rarely gave him a thought. They had far more in common than they could ever could have imagined. Both rode a roller coaster of wild ups but deeply sad downs. One day Joseph said, "I think I could enjoy my life if we could somehow find the middle between the highs and the lows. But, just as I think we have found the middle my Father comes in drunk with a bag of treasures he says he found and my Mother starts to cry and throw things at him. I guess there is no middle with the Samuels."

Missy wiped a tear, "The only highs in my family are my Dads. He is always overjoyed with the crops or his damn bull, Myron. He rarely looks at my Mother and she rarely pays him any mind. The lows are constant, he calls me a big fatso. He asks me what he did to fail me. At dinner time he complains if I ask for a second helping. Most nights I stay in the barn with my horse and cry. And, I do not want you coming to my defense with my Father. Stay away from him. He knows too many people, he would destroy you. Please promise me."

"I promise but can I still hate him?"

"No you can't hate him. That wouldn't be Christian."

"Sorry I don't know what a Christian is but I do know that a good many of those kids that teased you go to that Church downtown. So I'm not too impressed with Christians."

Missy sighed, "A Christian isn't going to church and following everybody. One of these days I need to set you down and tell you what a Christian really is. You will always be disappointed seeking God through other people."

Walking by his locker he saw a sign on the wall about the prom in two weeks turning to Missy standing in front of her locker, "Missy would you go to the prom with me?"

Missy turned with an angry look on her face, "Why would you want to take me to the prom? You think the fat girl will give it up easier?"

"Wow where did that come from?"

"I got asked to a party one year and the boy thought I would reward him for asking me. I had to fight the fool off and walk home. I'm not doing that again."

"Well I am not that boy. I just want to take you to the prom, so will you go with me?"

Looking into joseph's eyes she finally said, "Yes."

That night missy went home on cloud nine she was going to the prom. She announced to her Father and Mother over dinner the good news. Her Father chewed his roast for a bit before speaking, "No, you ain't going to the prom."

"Why not," Missy demanded.

"Because that boy is no good. He is the son of that thief William Samuels. That family is no good, they moved here because they got run out of Arlington. Besides, you know why he wants to take you, he just wants you to give it up. I ain't raising no damn child."

Missy left the table crying and as she ran from the room she heard her Father say, "Are all fat girls so moody?"

Missy knew she was going to the prom even if her Father said no, it would just take some extra planning. First, she told Joseph to pick her up down by the road at the end of their drive. Joseph knew why but it didn't seem to matter to him as he said, "So your Father doesn't want his daughter going out with the son of a thief?"

"Please don't be upset. I am sorry he is such a fool."

"No, I probably wouldn't want my daughter going out with someone from a family like mine. I'm not upset I will be at the end of the drive on prom night."

Second, over the next several days she took small bags of her makeup out to the barn and then when they were asleep she carried her dress out. She would get ready in the barn, it wasn't ideal but it was the only way. She knew her parents wouldn't check on her, they were used to her sleeping in the barn with her horse. So, the night of the prom she got ready and slowly made her way down the drive to where Joseph was waiting.

Joseph looked at Missy as she got in the car and said, "You look real pretty tonight."

The night was overwhelming for Missy, she had never had a boy dance with her or hold her. There were times in the evening she turned away from Joseph to wipe away the tears of joy. She kept telling herself, "This is the greatest night of my life."

Joseph took her home stopping the car at the drive way. Opening the door for her he looked into her eyes and bent forward and kissed her. As she walked away he said, "I had a great time."

Walking down the drive the tears kept falling, she had just had her first kiss after the best night of her life. Walking into the barn she went to her horse, Beauty, and held him close to her crying saying, "This was the greatest night of my life." Her horse licked the tears from her face as she held him tight.

CHAPTER THREE

Finally, as Joseph made his way through his senior year his Father decided it was time for Joseph to learn a trade, the family trade; looking for treasures that weren't tied down. As Joseph walked in the trailer from a full day of work he stopped surprised to see his Father sitting in his easy chair. William was normally at the bar getting drunk or already passed out in bed, but never sitting awake in his chair.

William spit in his tobacco juice in his cup as Joseph walked into the room. He had acquired the habit of chewing tobacco to calm his nerves while stealing. These days he had a cup in reaching distance at all times when home, otherwise he just spit where he felt like it, which was why he got banned from the Wal-Mart in Martin City.   The problem was even with a cup it there was a fifty percent chance he would miss thus leaving stains on the table next to his chair as well down the front of his shirt. Bertha often complained William was the nastiest man alive, no one ever disagreed.

Looking at Joseph William smiled, "Boy it is time you learned a real trade. You need to come with me tomorrow and I'll show you how to make money without sweat."

"I don't want to be a thief. I don't want to steal from people. I want a real life where I work and come home to a real family."

"What are you saying boy? You think you are going to get all those things? I got news for you, those people out there won't let you have what they got. The only way you'll get it is if you steal it. They have us pinned on the ground and the only way we can survive is to steal those fools blind."

"I don't believe that. I'm not giving up and being like you. Mom works to pay the bills with her back killing her. I work to help her and you just lay around drunk stealing a few things so you can pay for your bar tab. I'm not going to be like you."

William's face turned red as he got up from his chair dropping his cup, "You ungrateful little fool. No child of mine talks to me like that," as the tobacco juice oozed out the side of his mouth William swung his fist at Joseph. He missed and the force behind his effort caused him to lose balance. Laying on the floor feeling the effects of the beer he began to laugh, "Boy you're just like me. I told my old man off when I was about your age and now you continued the family tradition. Hell I hope you get what you want down the road. Help your old man up," he said raising his hand to Joseph.

Joseph reached for his hand as he pulled him up, "Pop I love you no matter what you do. I just want something better for myself." As William got to his feet he looked at his son and saw tears in his eyes, he suddenly he swung knocking Joseph down, "Boy, that's what those people will do to your foolish dreams," he said as he went down the hall to his bedroom.

Joseph got to his feet rubbing his chin realizing his Father had won the battle as he began to laugh, realizing in that moment he would never be like his Father. He would be his own man; at least his Father had taught him how not to be a man.

Life went on that year as Joseph and Bertha worked to keep the rent paid and food for the table. William continued uninterested in what they were doing as he found things to steal. Sunday was Bertha's day off, her day of rest. She always put on her best dress and walked across town to the Hillside Christian Church and sat alone on the sixth row next to the aisle. Sitting there that october Sunday she heard the whisper of a woman behind her, "Isn't that the wife of that drunk thief William Samuels. She has got some nerve coming here with him stealing from everybody."

As the preacher began Bertha wiped the tears from her eyes determined not to let anyone know she had heard what was said. This was her life and she was determined to live it to the end, a Christian, no matter what anyone thought. This was between her and God. As she walked out Reverend Lee took her aside, "Look people are broken. You need to know I love you and cherish you being here. Don't let anyone make you feel unwelcome."

Bertha was overcome as she hugged the Reverend and cried, "Thank you. You will never know what this means to me." Walking away she continued to wipe the tears as older woman grabbed her pulling her aside, "That Mary Margaret is just a judgmental old busy body. Don't forget you are loved by the believers here."

Walking away Bertha continued to cry as she realized she was loved. There were people out there that cared about her. She knew Joseph loved her but until today she thought no one else did. Her heart was full.

Walking into the trailer she looked around, no one was there. Joseph was at work and William was out getting drunk and stealing. Sitting down at the table she bowed her head and whispered a prayer, "Lord please help me. I can't go on much longer, this pain in my back is too great."

As she got up she felt a twitch in her heart as she slumped down in the chair. Joseph walked into the trailer at ten that night and saw his Mother slumped over the table, "Mom what is wrong? Talk to me." She said nothing, her life was over. Joseph called for an ambulance but when they walked into the trailer they knew there was nothing that could be done. Hearing that she was gone left a hole in Joseph's heart. Despite all that he had been through he knew she loved him. They never said it to each other but they both knew the other realized they were in this together. Now she was gone and he was left alone.

As they took her body to the morgue Joseph realized he needed to tell his Father. He found William at the Depot Bar drinking with his brother Randy. Walking up to the table he kept thinking how to tell his Father she was dead. Should he take him aside or should he be direct and tell him while he was at the table. Realizing his Father was a no nonsense kind of guy he decided to tell him at the table, "Pop, I have some bad news. Mom died today. I found her at the table and the medics came and said she was dead."

William looked at Randy and then Joseph, "Well boy that is too bad. We will miss her money."

"What, are you that unfeeling? How can you say something like that?"

"Boy don't get all sentimental. She was a fine woman but that is all. We hadn't been a real man and wife for a very long time. So she is gone, she is probably better off. Now, get out of here Randy and I are having a few drinks," William said as he waved Joseph to leave.

Joseph wanted to say something. He wanted to pull him out of his chair and beat him until he no longer existed. But he didn't, he just walked away and once outside he sat against the building crying.

Joseph took Monday off school to make arrangements for his Mother's funeral. He realized they had no money so he asked at the morgue what to do. They let him know the county would bury her at the City Cemetery if they had no money on Wednesday.   So with the burial for Wednesday he went to the Hillside Christian Church to ask the minister to say a few words over his Mother.

As Joseph walked into the minister's office he felt uneasy and out of place. He thought, 'This guy probably knows who I am and figures I am just another thief like my Father. These Christians are all judgmental.'

The minister got up and walked around the desk and grabbed Joseph in a great bear hug, "Son I am so sorry for your loss. Please have a seat and tell me what I can do."

Joseph struggled to keep himself from crying. There was something about this man that made him feel he was sincere that he really did care. "My Mom is to be buried on Wednesday at the city cemetery so I was wondering if you could say a word or two at that time. I don't have any money to pay you."

"City cemetery? Why there?"

"We don't have any money. So the county is going to bury her."

"That won't do."

"Ok if you don't want to do it, fine," Joseph said as he started to get up.

"No, no I didn't mean that. I meant she should be buried here at the church cemetery."

"But we don't have any money."

"Well the church has some money set aside for times like these," the minister said as he yelled for Gladys.

Gladys walked in the room, "What do you want?"

"Call the county morgue and tell them Bertha Samuels is to be buried in the Church's cemetery. We are paying for it," the minister said as he turned to Joseph, "I hope that is ok."

Joseph smiled for the first time in a very long time, "Yes that is great."

Joseph didn't bother to tell his Father of the funeral. There was no reason to hear how he didn't care. So that Wednesday Joseph said good bye as the minister said a few words. The one thing Joseph could not get out his mind the preacher said was, "She was a believer despite all that the world threw at her."

Later that night after work he found his Father once again sitting in his easy chair with his cup in hand asleep. The tobacco juice ran down his cheek as he laid there snoring. Joseph tried to shut the door quietly not wanting to wake his Father, but the creek in the door woke him, "Well boy you are home," his Father said as he raised up in his chair putting the cup of juice down.

"Yes, it has been a long day," Josephs starting for the bedroom.

"Wait, we need to talk."

"I don't feel like talking. I'm going to bed."

"Like hell you are. Sit down on that couch, we need to talk."

"No."

William reached around his back and pulled out a gun, "I said sit down. If you don't I'll put a hole in you boy. You know I would."

Joseph looked at the gun and the drunk anger in his eyes and said as he sat down, "Ok, let's talk."

"They told me they buried Bertha at the church cemetery today."

"Yes, that is right. I didn't tell you because I figured you didn't care to go."

"That's right but who in the hell decided to bury her there. I ain't paying no church for a plot. You had no right to do that. You better be paying for it, because I ain't."

"The church paid for it. We don't owe anything."

"That's worse fool. Those holier than thou people will have that over our heads," William said waving the gun at Joseph.

"It was my doing so it will be over my head. You're not a part of it."

"Ok, I just ain't paying for that woman to be buried."

Joseph started to get up, "So we are done here. I'm going to bed."

William shouted as he fired a shot next to Joseph's arm into the couch, "No! We ain't done. You stay right there boy."

"Are you crazy? You could have hit me."

"If you get up again I will. I am tired of you thinking your better than me. So, you are going to listen and do what I say from now on. Your Bertha ain't around to protect you. You need to give me your checks each week so I can pay the bills."

"I'll pay the bills. You'll just drink the money away."

William looked at Joseph with hate in his eyes and fired the gun again just beyond Joseph's arm, "No, you will do what I say. I expect you to give me those checks each week. You understand boy? You see when I see you I see Bertha and her praying for me and all that stupid church stuff all these years. I hated her for it and I hate you because you are just like her. You think you're better than me well you ain't. You'll end up at the bottom just like me one day because those people out there ain't going to let you get up from the bottom."

"Ok, are we done? Can I get up now without you shooting me."

"I don't know why we don't see what happens," William said as he laughed.

Slowly Joseph got up and started down the hall when he heard the gun shot. He stood there a second wondering if he had been shot but realizing he had not he looked back at his father. He was sitting in the chair laughing at the look on Joseph's face, "Boy you thought you was a dead man. Just remember that if you try anything in the future.

It was the middle of October and Joseph was going to school and working at the grocery store. Missy and him still sat together every day at lunch and talked about their lives. Most of their talks were about the lives they spent at home but today was different. Missy had a big smile on her face when she sat down at the lunch table, "Guess what?"

"I have no idea. Just tell me."

"I just found out I got a scholarship to Belmont University in Nashville."

"Wow, that is great. I am so happy for you." As Joseph reached out his hand touching her hand smiling he continued, "That really makes me happy. I am so proud of you."

"It's funny when I told my parents last night my Dad said nothing and my Mother said 'You need to buy something decent to wear besides those rags.' It is nice to have someone in my life who really cares for me."

"There is one thing you can be certain of, I care for you. We may have miserable lives at home but those lives aren't going to mold us. We are not going to be those people. We are going to survive the life they have given us and make a great life for ourselves."

Missy looked at joseph for a moment and then began to cry as she came around the table to hug him. As she hugged him a teacher tapped her on the shoulder, "You are not supposed to do that in here." She let go and just smiled, nothing was going to take her smile away, she was certain Joseph was right they were not going to be like their parents.

CHAPTER FOUR

William sat at the Depot Bar with a beer in one hand and his cup in the other. The stains on his shirt were a reminder of how poor he was at hitting the cup. He had been sitting in the booth in the back of the bar for three hours now pondering the dilemma he faced. Without Bertha bringing in her check there was not enough money to pay the bills. He thought, 'That spoiled boy won't quit school and get a real job to pay the bills so it is up to me. This is a bad situation to be in.'

Stealing bits and pieces of things left unattended was not going to pay the bills, he needed to up the ante. He needed to steal bigger and better things, but how and where was he going to find anything worth stealing he kept asking himself. As he considered his dire situation Maggie walked up from behind him, "Well how you been?"

"Sis, I ain't seen you in a long while."

"Yeah it has been since last New Years' Eve. You remember you and Bernard got drunk and shot the plastic reindeer in the neighbors' lawn," she laughed as she sat down.

"Yeah I think we also shot plastic baby Jesus and the wise men up at the church," William said as he grabbed his beer laughing.

"Yes that was an out of control night; a good deal of fun. We'll have to do it again real soon."

"I hear you made some more money this year."

"Yes, I collected $12,500 from the Wilmington Mall and $7,500 from Stop Eleven." Maggie was a true Samuels who had found a use of her talent of getting attention. For years she had fallen when she felt there was a need to draw attention her way. Once she was upset her husband was flirting with the cashier at Walmart so she took one of her dives to get attention. The manager was overly concerned because someone had spilled a soda not far from where she fell. Realizing the manager was upset she saw an opportunity to make money. $15,000 later Maggie realized her talent was not only an attention grabber but was also a money maker. Ever since she had sought places with a spill or uneven floor and boom she hit the ground. She had the amazing good luck that her husband was filming her just before the fall. Maggie's business was slip and fall and settle.

"I think I need to get into that line of work."

"You would be no good at it. It takes talent to sell it. I have that talent. On the other hand, I couldn't steal things, you can. So I guess those folks at the church are right, God gives us different talents," she said as she laughed.

"You want a beer?"

"No get me a scotch on the rocks."

"Ok, but you are buying."

"So you need to make some money?"

"Yes, Bertha is dead and I need money to pay the bills."

"I heard about Bertha. I figured she would leave you sooner or later. Well brother you need to be stealing cars. That is where the money is."

"What am I going to do with them?"

"Look I know a little about the business but I can't tell you how I know, you not knowing means they can't get it out of you if you get caught."

"I understand but what can you tell me?"

"I think you need to talk to Randy. He'll help you. Then maybe both of you can make some real money. I'm going," she said as she gulped down her scotch and just as she started to walk away she turned around and leaned over the table, "Don't try the slip and fall thing that is mine. If you do, things will get real bad for you. Love you brother. I'll tell Randy you are waiting to see him, he'll be by in a few."

Sitting there William laughed to himself, 'My sister threatening me. She's a real Samuels. Just like Mom.'

Realizing he was going to be there a while he ordered a hamburger and fries and another Miller. Sitting back in the booth he wondered what Randy would have in mind for them to do. No matter what he had in mind he told himself, 'I ain't going to take too many big chances. I don't want to go to prison.'

Randy had spent his life being between chased by the police and being caught by the police. He had served three six month sentences in the county jail for shoplifting and five years for stealing a car. He was a real Samuels playing his part on the stage of life drawing attention to himself, which was not a particularly good attribute for a thief. It did not matter he was a Samuels and he was compelled to make a splash of the stage of life. His first shoplifting he picked up twenty bags of gum and stood outside the door handing them to people as they entered the store. The second shoplifting he tried stealing a TV while his sister was slipping and falling at a Walmart. He walked out of the store as the manager and employees were calling an ambulance telling everyone how easy it was to steal from there. By the time he got caught for the third shoplifting he had gotten smarter but people had gotten smarter as well so they kept a good eye out for him. The car thief was another foolish effort on his part. He tried stealing the sheriff's wife's car.

As Randy walked into the bar he saw William in the back booth spitting in his cup. Walking up to the table he looked at the spit that had missed the cup and landed on the fries William was eating, "You are the most disgusting person I know, and I spent some time with some really disgusting people in prison."

"Yeah well I may be disgusting but I ain't no jail bird."

"Not yet but the way you are going they are going to catch up to you real soon."

"How you figure."

"Everybody in town knows you and I are stealing all the time, so they are watching us. One of these days they will catch you stealing a lawnmower or bike on a security camera and off you go. The sad thing is you are putting yourself at risk for nickel and dime stuff fool."

Feeling a little hurt by his brother's remarks William sat up, "Look I have managed all these years to steal and not get caught. I don't need a lecture from you on the art of stealing. Don't forget I am the older one here."

"Don't get all sensitive. I am just trying to tell you if you are going to risk going to jail stealing you need to be risking it for something worth stealing."

"Ok, what is worth stealing?"

Randy leaned over the table and lowered his voice, "Look Arnold Richman has a boat load of money in a safe at his house. We could live a good life off of it."

"How do you know that?"

"When I got out of prison I worked on Arnold's farm for a summer. He caught me smoking in the barn and fired me. He took me up to his office in the back of his home and opened the safe and pulled out a wad of money to pay me. I never seen so much money as there was in that safe."

"Wow, but how do we know he still has money in the safe?"

"Look the crops are being picked right now, he will have his corn and bean money. The safe will be full of money. They have the Fall Festival Dinner to celebrate the harvest at his church down the road from him. We wait until the family leaves and goes to the church and then we go and get the money."

"But how we gonna get the safe open?"

"Look I have it all planned out. I have two sticks of dynamite I picked up at the quarry if we can't open it we blow it. But it would be better to carry it out of there and blow it later. The decision we have to make is if it is too heavy or not. If it is we just blow it there."

"Wait you picked up two sticks of dynamite?"

"Ok, stole."

"But we don't have a truck to put the safe in."

"Well getting a truck is the first step. We can't use a truck we have stolen so we need to steal a few cars to get enough money to buy a truck. Look this is our chance to have something. What do you say?"

William was reluctant to became a thief of anything that would get him more than county jail time, but maybe Randy was right.

CHAPTER FIVE

Randy and William made their way over to Port City and after a while found an old Ford Escort with the keys in it. Randy jumped in and drove off to Billy Ryan's Parts Shop. Billy's place was out of town down a narrow stone drive in the middle of the woods. There at the end of the drive was an old farm house and a pole building with a sign across the top that said, "Billy's Parts."

The owner, Billy Ryan, was a six foot five man with a beard that hung down to his chest and tattoos down his neck and arms. He has spent seven years in Federal Prison for running drugs for a group from Guatemala and often said, "There will be dead bodies if they try to put me in prison again." No one doubted Billy wasn't serious after all there were rumors of people who hadn't been seen since crossing Billy.

The two got of their cars and approached the building when they saw Billy standing with a shotgun across his chest. "What you boys wantin'?"

"Billy it is me Randy. I got you another car."

Billy took stolen cars from those he trusted and turned them into parts overnight. The next morning the parts were on the way to a dealer in Wisconsin and any parts with numbers that could be traces were headed to the dump. Randy's wife worked at the dump so she took the parts to a hole at the dump that would be filled by evening.

Looking at the car Billy laughed, "You brought me a Ford Escort? Hell I don't need it. But I'll take it; here is $500."

William looked at the money Billy handed him, "Are you trying to screw me?"

Billy looked up, "Look, you brought me a Ford Escort. Hell I can't make money on it. Bring me something decent and I'll pay you more. Now one more thing if you bring a car here again and complain I'll take this here shotgun and blow your damn brains out, you understand? I ain't puttin' up with no complainin'. So if you can't keep your mouth shut don't be bringin' anything here again."

William backed up and smiled, "Feller I ain't complainin' I'm happy with the money. I'll bring you somethin' better."

William and Randy walked to their car as they got in William said, "Did you see the money that dude had in that drawer?"

"Yes, but that fellow isn't the kind of fellow to mess around with."

"I know. I ain't gonna try stealin' his money. I just want to have that kind of money. That old farmer might just do the trick."

That evening Joseph walked into the trailer after a day of school and the grocery store with his legs aching to find William passed out in his chair with tobacco juice oozing down his chin. In his left hand was an half empty can of Pabst Blue Ribbon which he had been drinking out of and spitting in as he got drunker. The room was filled with the smell of William since he hadn't bothered taking a bath in the last three weeks. As Joseph started by William woke, "Hey boy your old man is going be rich."

"I'm sure you are," Joseph said continuing down the hall to his bedroom.

William yelled trying to get up but falling back in the chair, "You'll be sorry you weren't in on this boy." There was no answer as Joseph got in bed with his clothes on and shut his eyes. Laying there under the covers he wished there was a better place for him, a better life. He kept asking, 'Is this the best I can do? Is this the life I will have?' As the questions ran through his mind he slowly slipped into sleep.

The next day at school he and Missy sat talking about their lives. Somehow sharing their misery made life manageable for them. Missy talked about her Father Arnold Richman a stout ordinary looking man standing six feet with a round face that was two toned. The lower part of his face was red from the sun while the top of his head was white from having been shaded his entire life from the sun by his John Deer hat. His lips turned down in what appeared to be a constant scowl with large lips and a pouting mouth. His arms were muscular from the many years of farm work but as time passed and he ate too much home cooking he was getting punchy with his belly slipping over his belt.

Arnold had lived his life with one goal to have the best and to be the best. Starting out on a small farm he had over the years built it into the finest farm in Lewis County. He was a driven man who never bothered to turn off his drive. As a result he was driven to be considered the best Christian at the Mt. Kathryn Church just a few miles down the road. He was an elder on the church board helping to pick the minister and determining the direction the church should go.

Because of his drive he was considered the most important person around in terms of political office. If you wanted a county office you needed to go to Arnold, he was the king maker for Lewis County. Judges and prosecutors had been to Arnold's farm seeking his endorsement. Once they got in office Arnold never let them forget it, he often needed favors and if they wanted to win the next election they would give him what he wanted.

His farm was the biggest in Southern Indiana with a white board fence marking the boundaries of the farm. Across the entry to the drive to his home stood a giant sign that said, "Richman Farms." Down the long paved drive was an old two story farm house built in 1845 by Silas McDonald an Irish immigrant who settled here to build a better life. The county history says Silas' wife died giving birth to her first child Liam who 16 years later shot his Father, Silas, and then ran off to the West where he was shot in a bar room fight with Jesse James. Arnold's Father bought the farm from an old man who couldn't get anything to grow in the Southern Indiana red clay. Arnold an only child inherited the farm when his Father got hit in the head by the old mule. Arnold's mother had died years earlier so overnight Arnold became the owner of the farm. Over the years he added to the farm buying out neighbors who couldn't make a go of it.

Arnold was on the third row right side of the church every Sunday often saying amen louder than anyone. For Arnold there were two worlds, the church world and the world outside the church. In the church world he was a devote believer reading the Bible and sharing his faith with anyone who bothered to ask or got caught by him for a moment. In the world outside the church he said, "It was win or lose. Be the victor or the loser." Arnold told the Sheriff one afternoon, "Winning is what it is all about. There are two groups of people, winners and losers. I intend to be a winner and in this world it means you have to do what is necessary, and I'm prepared to do just that."

Arnold was so sure of himself and his way of living he never questioned the fact his religion never made it out of the church into his world. He knew his way of living was the right way and anyone who thought differently was about to get a big surprise. When he took over his family farm the neighbor farmer was Eric Moon who had farmed his 200 acres for twenty years barely getting by. Arnold found out Eric was behind on his bank loan so Arnold pushed the banker to pressure him to either sell or be sued. Eric chose to sell and Arnold was the buyer at seventy percent of what it was worth. It was the Arnold way using whatever he could use to win. He often said at church, "The Lord helps those who help themselves."

Every year he sought to have the highest yield of corn and beans and the highest quality of the beef. He worked all year constantly studying methods to increase yield and deliver grain with low moisture content to the local elevator. His real pride and joy however was his bull, Myron. Myron was an Angus bull that had, over the years, fetched a high price for his semen. Arnold sold Myron's semen all over the country at high prices due to his strong bloodline. Over his life Myron had made Arnold a little over a million dollars but sadly he was getting close to the end of the line at seven years old. Nevertheless, Arnold was unwilling to let go of his money maker so he continued to collect his semen and collected the big checks although the quality was slowly decreasing. Arnold gave Myron a special place by the barn where he was fed only the best feed and treated like royalty. Most folks thought Arnold liked Myron more than his wife or Missy; most folks were right.

Arnold may have said he wanted to be the best at everything but he drew the line when it came to being the best husband or father. His wife, Rachel, accepted her place on the list of important things mainly because she didn't much care for Arnold. Rachel had come to town taking a job as a third grade teacher in the local school. As she settled into town she examined the prospects for a husband and found the field fairly small. Her first target was a young farmer named Lee Cole. He had deep blue eyes and blonde hair that seem to glow against his perfect tan skin. He stood six foot four and until Rachel he had not been caught by any of the ladies in town. Rachel thought she was just the woman to win his heart and after some effort managed to get a dinner date. It was the second date that things finally fell apart. As they sat down Lee said he had to go to the bathroom, just as he had the first time they were there. And, just like the first time she noticed the waiter followed him to the bathroom. Fifteen minutes later he reappeared at the table pushing his shirt into his pants as he sat down. Rachel paused a moment and then said, "I have two things to say to you. First, what you did tonight and on our last date is rude and dishonorable."

Lee pulled his chair forward, "What are you talking about?"

"You know perfectly well what I am talking about you and the waiter are having a little fling in the bathroom. I am not stupid and I don't appreciate being treated like I am. And, I don't like you disrespecting me. Now as to the second thing. It is a miserable way to live life trying to be what you think others want you to be. You are living a lie and it is an awful way to live. Just be yourself, be who you are. Some won't like you for it and some will. Quit being a lying coward." With that Rachel began to get up.

"Wait, don't go. I am sorry you are right please stay and have dinner with me."

"No, I am not staying and you need to know just saying you are sorry isn't enough. I will get over it but I will never respect you if you continue to live this way." Rachel walked away calling a fellow teacher to pick her up.

The second person she dated was Warren Moody the junior minister at the church. He had been in the job for 22 years. Now at the age of 42 he seemed a bit silly with his brown hair pulled back in a ponytail using the current slang words from time to time. Rachel had met him at church and agreed to go out with him although he was 18 years older. On their first date Warren stopped the car at the drive way and asked her to pray with him. He said, "Let's pray for God's guidance as to where we should eat." They prayed for a few moments and suddenly he announced God was calling them to the local steak house. As they sat down at the table and began to look at the menu once again he asked that they pray to see what God wanted them to eat, he was pleased to report a sirloin steak was God's choice for him.

The second and third date followed the same routine. Interestingly God kept picking restaurants with steaks. On the third date Warren walked Rachel to the door stopping there he said, "Let's pray to see if God wants me to kiss you." As he bent his head Rachel exclaimed, "God said no," as she opened and slammed the door in his face.

At a community business meeting she met Dillion Jones, the owner of the Jones funeral home. Dillion wore black suits with black ties on their dates and had a constant look of sympathy pasted on his face. He was short and balding with a round face and belly, but he was single in a place where there weren't many single men. His dates always involved his telling of the newest customers of the funeral home. There was Billy Squire who was mangled in a car wreck on a county road who Dillion was able to reconstruct so they could have an open casket. Then there was Lilly Newman who had laid dead for three weeks before the smell caused anyone to be concerned. The story that finally ended their dating was the Frank Anderson story. According to Dillion Frank had got caught bedding his wife's sister a couple years ago so one night his wife took a knife and cut his penis off. Frank lived with the loss of his friend for two years but finally he couldn't take it any longer so he put a gun to head and blew a hole clean through. As he finished his story he asked, "Do you want to see a photo of what his thing looked like cut off like that," as he offered her his phone.

Rachel looked with horror in her eyes at Dillion, "No, please no."

Next was Arnold, a good looking muscular man with the best farm in the county. He had money and he had looks, she decided earlier on he was the one she would marry and she did.

In the early days Rachel struggled to compete against Arnold's other love, himself but finally she realized Arnold would never love anyone as much as he loved himself. Arnold saw Rachel as a trophy that was to be by his side at church and social events but otherwise she was forgotten and put aside. She thought a baby would change him, make him more mature and concerned about someone other than himself. She was wrong, Arnold liked the baby not because of the baby but because of how it made him look, a Godly successful young man with a family.

As Missy grew older she became a disappointment to both Arnold and Rachel. She became a round tubby baby that soon turned into a fat little ten year old girl. Rachel tried taking her to the gym as well as not letting her eat extra helpings of food but she kept getting fatter. Finally Rachel decided when Missy was 12 she would have the cook give her half portions. Every night, Missy would storm away from the table crying because they wouldn't let have more to eat. Finally the cook could not watch it go on any longer so she started to give Missy food to take to the barn to eat behind their backs. This went on months until Arnold found Missy eating in the barn. They fired the cook and got another that promised to obey their rules.

By the time Missy was 13 they gave up as they saw her getting fatter not slimmer. The new cook walked in one night and told Arnold and Rachel she quit as she said, "The reason that girl is fat is because she is miserable. You both treat her awful and she goes to school and they tease her there and you do nothing about it because you blame her not the kids in school. I won't work here any longer."

Arnold looked up from his dinner and said, "Good bye." Rachel said nothing as she picked at the pears on her plate.

Frustrated Arnold often said, "Missy you are fat. You will never get a man looking like that." Missy spent most of her time in the barn with her horse. Being away from her Father and Mother meant being away from their insults. She named her horse Beauty, something she wanted to be but wasn't, she thought.

Beauty was an Appaloosa horse with great coloring. Missy was 13 the day she saw her horse at an auction. She fell in love immediately and as her Father bid on another horse she asked, "Daddy buy that horse for me, please. I'll take good care of her."

Arnold stopped bidding on a quarter horse for a moment and looked at his daughter and laughed, "Hell that horse isn't strong enough to carry you around. You would break her back."

Missy started to cry but then determination took hold of her and she said, "Fine I'll buy her."

Arnold barely looked at her, "Fine buy her with your money." Arnold moved a few seats away from Missy embarrassed that people would see him with her.

Missy had money she had saved from selling tomatoes at the Farmer's Market. "Ok I'll buy her myself." So she did. Missy spent her evenings talking with Beauty sitting by her in the stall. There were times she fell asleep next to Beauty and would wake in the morning realizing no one noticed her absence from the home.

Arnold was one of those people who saw something entirely different in the mirror than the rest of the world. He saw a handsome man with muscular arms and wavy hair with little bits of gray around the temples. He didn't see the belly that was slowly slipping over his belt line or his crooked nose or his drooping eyes or the fact his hair line was receding showing more of his bright white forehead. He often remarked, "Everyone loves Arnold Richman."

As Rachel gave up competing for Arnold's attention she was lured by those who showed her attention. Judge Stevens found her to be a beautiful woman and his attention was all she wanted so she started driving over to Fremont to room six every Thursday afternoon. The irony was not lost on the Judge. Arnold had helped him get the job as Judge and because of that he could take Thursday afternoons off to enjoy Rachel. Rachel knew nothing would come of their meetings. The Judge didn't love her; she just liked the attention and they both enjoyed the forbidden sex. Leaving the Judge each time she drove home to Arnold and watched while the maid prepared his meal as if nothing had happened. Rachel often fantasized about putting a little rat poison in his mashed potatoes while the cook wasn't looking.

Getting married Arnold's biggest fear was Rachel would be able to get part of his money or part of the farm. He told her, "If we are going to marry you need to sign a prenuptial. I won't have anyone taking what I have worked so hard to get from me." She agreed to sign it as well as the six amendments prepared over the years in which she agreed again and again if they got a divorce she would get nothing other than her car and he would nothing of hers. Arnold often laughed when he came to the part about him getting part of what she had, "hell you ain't got nothing. Your parents are dirt poor. You got nothing I would ever want."

What Arnold never understood Rachel was never worried about getting his money she was worried about him getting a part of her money. Her parents had been poor farmers in Southern Illinois in a three room house. They owned five acres and her father helped farm the large farm next to them. Arnold was so busy feeling superior to them and Rachel he didn't take time to understand the farm they worked on was Rachel's Grandparents. When they first dated she tried telling Arnold about her Grandparents but he was too busy talking about his favorite subject, himself. If he had paid attention he would have known her Grandparents had a 500 acre farm and 17 oil wells stretching from the Indiana border to the Missouri State line in Southern Illinois. And he would have been interested in knowing Rachel was the sole heir to all of it after her parents. Her Grandparents died seven years ago and her parents three years ago in a car accident. Again, Arnold was too busy being in love with himself to pay attention to what was going with Rachel. Rachel traveled back home for the funerals alone since Arnold was too busy with the farm to care or accompany her.

Rachel spent much of her time the phone dealing with the farmer she hired to run the farm and the oil man who took care of the wells. Her bank account in a small Irvington, Illinois bank grew and grew and Arnold had no idea, she was worried about him getting her money.

So, when the prenuptial idea came up Rachel was more than happy to sign and resign to make sure he got none of her money. She knew one day she would leave him, she hadn't figured out what day that would be. She told herself it was because of Missy but that was not true, she often asked herself, 'Why am I still here with this man. I am just a fool.'

The harvest season was a busy time as Arnold pushed the boys working for him to get the crops in before rain. He was determined to get the best production to the elevator before the rest of the farmers in the county and most years he did. None of the other farmers in the county saw it as a competition but Arnold did and he was determined to win.

This was a particularly rough year for Arnold; Myron was clearly coming to the end of his good semen years. There were not going to be many pay days ahead for Myron's semen, but Arnold felt sorrow for his prize bull. He watched as Myron didn't seem to have the will to get it up for the new stock that Arnold let him wonder around. Determined Myron would not be mistreated he kept him in the pen next to the barn feeding him the best grain and letting him wander over to see the ladies from time to time even if he had trouble making good on his advances. Rachel often laughed, "You feel sorry for that damn fool bull because he is just like you. You can't get it up these days."

At the end of the harvest time was the Harvest Festival Dinner at the church where everyone brought their special dishes and enjoyed talking about the harvest. Arnold knew Rachel wouldn't pitch in anything worth eating so he bought some pies from the Amish down the road to take. One year Rachel had made homemade ice cream for the Harvest Dinner but in her effort to make everyone healthy she had left out sugar in the recipe. It was a disaster, Arnold had to go around the room picking up everyone's bowl of ice cream and apologizing for his wife. He would not let that happen again.

Arnold looked forward to the Harvest Dinner because he could tell the others how well his crops had done and give the prayer. He worked weeks on his prayers, wanting to say just the right things in the right way and in the right order. It was his opportunity to once again be in the spotlight. The problem was he kept the spotlight on him so long some had to sit down. Leo Goldman a small farmer down the road started a pool on how many times Arnold would say, "Heavenly Father." Billy Mitchell won it last year guessing 23, he actually said it 24 times. Everyone wanted someone else to give the prayer but no one was brave enough to tell Arnold, so he once again was going to give it and he was sure it would be his best. But worse than the prayers was his effort to one up everyone as they talked about their crops. His yields were better than theirs, his moisture count less, and because of his equipment he used less help getting the crops to the elevator down the way.

CHAPTER SIX

The grocery store closed early so everyone could go to the Harvest Festival Dinner, so Joseph had the evening off. He made his way to the trailer exhausted from a week of school and work. Walking into trailer the silence was welcomed, there was no drunk William just an empty trailer. Joseph sat down on the couch to rest a moment when he heard a truck pull up, 'Oh no drunk fool is home.'

Moments later William and Randy stumbled into the trailer laughing with a case of Pabst Blue Ribbon. Before they could get inside Randy laughed, "Boy, your old man is somethin', took this case of beer from the cooler while I talked to the bartender. He stole it right out from under his nose. I ain't ever seen nothin' like it. The dumb fool didn't know we was stealing a case of beer," as he finished Randy fell against the trailer wall laughing slowly falling to the floor as he heaved in laughter.

"What can I say, I am the best damn thief in this part of the country," Joe laughed before going on, "Look we need to do some planning here fellows. I am good at stealing because I think ahead and we need to think ahead and plan to take that dumb farmers' money."

Irritated by the end of the quiet Joseph asked, "What farmer are you stealing from?"

Randy trying to regain an upright position said, "Arnold Richman. We goinna steal that old farmer's money right out of his safe."

"Wait, that is Missy's Father. You can't steal from her Father. I won't let you."

William walked over to Joseph sitting on the couch and pointed his finger at him, "Who in the hell do you think you are? You have no right telling us who we can steal from. Just because you got a thing for that fat girl don't mean nothing to us."

"Look you damn drunk I'm not going to let you talk that way about her and I'm not going to let you steal from her family," Joseph said as he stood up looking down at his Father.

As Joseph approached William the sound of a gun shot rang in the trailer. Looking back at Randy they saw him with a gun having shot a hole in the floor. As he pointed the gun at Joseph he said, "Boy you sure ain't no Samuels. You ain't gonna stop us or tell us what to do. Now trust me if I have to I'll put three holes in that hard head of yours and bury you in the woods."

William looked at Joseph, "Yeah boy we are tired of dancing around you. Just because you are soft we ain't and we will put you in the ground if you don't watch yourself."

"You both are drunk fools."

"Yeah well we may be but we are the ones with the gun pointed at your head," Randy said.

Looking at Joseph Randy said, "Sit down fool your Pop and I need to talk things over."

"Look we can't leave him here. He will call Missy or the police. We could just shoot him and dump his body, but he is family," Randy said as he wiped his face.

"Yeah, I know. He is a big disappointment but I don't like the idea of killing him, so why don't we tie him up and put him in the back of the truck?"

"Good idea. That way he can't call anyone."

"Where did you get a truck?

"None of your business boy," William said.

"Hell I'll tell the fool. We stole a Cambry in Covington and took it to Barry's shop and traded for the truck. He cuts up vehicles and sells them to a fellow in Wisconsin. Your old man and I aren't so dumb after all, are we?"

Joseph shook his head as his Father and Randy tied him up, "You two are really idiots."

Randy said tape his mouth shut as he hit Joseph in the stomach. William thought a moment and realized he needed to hit him as well so he hit him in the mouth. "Now boy maybe you will show your elders some respect. Your Mom was too soft on you."

They carried him out to the truck and shoved him into the bed of the truck and started down the road with a beer between their legs. In the back Joseph thought about being in Covington the other day picking up some supplies for the grocery store. He had stopped at the diner to get a sandwich when he overheard the waitress telling about her car being stolen. She said she had saved for three years to buy the car and now it was gone. He realized these old fools had stolen that poor girls' car, he thought, 'Another reason to hate them.'

Randy pulled the truck into Moonlight lane so they could watch for Arnold and his family to drive by, then they would go and make off with the money. They were too drunk to realize they stood out parked along the side of the road at night. Sitting there with the lights off they watched as people slowed down as they drove by looking at them. William wondered, "Do you think they recognize us?"

"It don't matter. There is nothing wrong with being parked here."

"Yeah I guess you're right. I sure wish Arnold and his family would come by."

As they sat there old man Sanders and his family stopped, rolling his window down he yelled, "You fellows need help?"

Randy yelled, "No, the engine just over heated and we are lettin' it cool. Thanks."

As old man Sanders drove off William said, "This may very well be the dumbest idea ever. We are sitting here while everyone drives by. They will take about ten minutes to solve this crime. Two damn drunks hatching a foolish scheme. I should never have agreed to this."

"You always were the soft one. Always afraid to do anything don't back out now," Randy said as he took another drink of his bottle.

They sat there in silence except for William spitting in his plastic cup and Randy sucking down his beer from time to time. Joseph struggled in the bed of the pickup trying to loosen the knots the drunks had tied. Much to his surprise they were far better knots than he had expected they were capable of.

At the Arnold house Rachel was spending her time looking in the mirror upset with the way her hair fell across her forehead and the dress was just not right, it made her look, 'Too common,' she thought. Arnold was trying on his blue jacket and noticing it didn't fit across his chest like it did last year. Oh well he thought, 'I still am what the women want.' Getting downstairs he yelled, "Come on I have to be there to give my prayer."

Rachel threw her comb at the mirror and marched down the steps with fire in her eyes, "I am walking out if your damn foolish prayer goes on and on like it did last year. Hell nobody wants to hear your nonsense."

Arnold looked back at Rachel as he opened the door, "Everyone wants to hear what I have to say. Everyone likes Arnold Richman."

Rachel just laughed as she walked out the door. Looking on the porch she asked, "What are you to do with those stupid gas grill tanks?"

"I'm going to leave them there for now."

Rachel had complained for some time about the wood fireplace in the family room so in order to get some peace and quiet Arnold agreed to make it a gas fireplace. The problem was he refused to pay the gas company for a large propane tank. As he said, "Those folks up in Covington City don't know who I am. They want to make me pay for that damn tank. I'll fix them I'll just use gas grill tanks." So now he had four gas grill tanks sitting on the back porch in his way in order to keep from paying the propane company for a large tank.

Looking at the tanks Rachel said, "They look awful. Folks are going to think white trash live here. When are you going to hook them up?" looking around Rachel went on, "Where is Missy?"

Arnold shrugged his shoulders, "In the barn with her horse probably."

"Didn't you tell her to get ready?"

"No, I figured she wouldn't want to go so I left her alone."

"You old fool. You are ashamed of her that's why you didn't say anything."

"I noticed you didn't say anything to her. And, yes I'm embarrassed she is so fat. You think she would show some pride in herself for once."

"Oh well let's go," Rachel said as she went out the door. She stopped looking at the four propane tanks on the porch again, "Why are you so damn cheap?"

As they made their way down the road they passed a truck sitting with its lights off at Moonlight Lane. Arnold looked at the truck, "That is that no good thief William Samuels. He is going to try stealing something."

As he turned the car around Rachel asked, "What are you doing? We are going to be late."

"That thief is going to steal my propane tanks I just know it."

"So what are you going to do, guard them?"

"No, I'm going to put them up so he can't get to them."

Back at the house Arnold quickly made his way to the porch carrying the propane tanks inside and stacking them in his office. Getting back in the car Rachel asked, "Aren't you going to get your daughter?"

"No, why would I do that?"

"You think William Samuels is going to try stealing from you and your daughter is in the barn. She might be in danger."

"Nobody is going to bother her. Haven't you seen her lately? Hell they would run from her."

"Well at least go tell her to be looking out for them."

Getting out the car Arnold walked down to the barn, inside Missy was sitting talking to her horse. Arnold shook his head, "Why in the world do you waste your time talking to that dumb horse. She probably wishes you would give her some peace and quiet. Anyway, we saw William Samuels down the road so he may show up here to steal something so get your shotgun ready. Make sure you still have birdshot in there so from a distance you won't kill him but will make it painful to sit down so shoot him in the back side."

Missy pointed to the end of the stall where her shotgun was and without looking at her Father said, "I will take care of things here, you go and have fun. Bring me back something to eat."

Arnold shook his head and walked out without another word making his way to the car. Rachel and him drove down the road and saw William was still there but Arnold kept going after all he was going to miss his prayer.

William watched as Arnold drove by the second time, "What is up with that fool."

"His wife probably forgot something. Wives are like that. I had one once and she was forgetting just about everything all the time. Hell she even forgot to come home and I never saw her again," Randy laughed.

Finally William said, "its been long enough he ain't turnin' around again, let's go get rich."

Stopping in front of the drive that lead to the farm house they pulled off the road getting out they checked the bed of the truck to make sure Joseph was still tied securely. As they started to walk away Randy went back to the truck and put his gun to Joseph's head, "Look boy you try getting loose I'll put a bullet in that head of yours."

As William and Randy creeped down the drive Randy handed one of the sticks of dynamite, "Here put this in your back pocket I ain't got room for two."

"You think we will need them?"

"I don't know. I sure wish I had brought a beer with me."

Hearing them walk away Joseph began to struggle trying to loosen the knots. He felt he was making some headway but knew once he got to a point he had to be sure to get free before they got back. If they saw he had tried to get loose they probable would do what they promised, put a hole in his head.

As William and Randy walked down the drive they couldn't help but think how easy this was. Randy turned to William and laughed, "No dogs no security, the way the way I see it the farmer is wanting us to steal the money."

Looking back at Randy with a puzzled look William said, "How you figure that."

"We steal the money and he turns into the insurance twice as much. He ends up even richer. We're doing him a favor."

"Yeah we are."

Missy heard the truck down stopping at the end of drive and she knew something was about to happen. She watched from the barn as two men slowly walked down the drive. As they grew closer to the back of the house she grabbed her shotgun and crawled out to the fence line behind the watering trough and waited. She knew from there she would have a clean shot at them if they attempted to break in the house.

As they reached the back porch Randy said pointing to the back of the house, "His safe is in there in his office."

"How are we going to get in?" William asked as he looked at the door.

"Simple," Randy said as he took a board and broke the window.

Looking back at William he began to crawl through the window, "We are about to be rich."

William laughed as he began to follow, "Yes this is our lucky day."

Missy was reluctant to fire failing to pull the trigger when they broke the window and began to crawl through. Finally she felt she had no choice so she brought the gun to her shoulder aimed and pulled the trigger. She kept telling herself, 'At this distance the buck shot will fill his ass with buck shot and get his attention but It won't kill the fool.'

Joseph continued to work at the knots finally getting one to come loose freeing a hand. With the free hand he loosen another and another until he was free. Pulling the duct tape from his face he winced at the pain as it pulled skin away from his upper lip. Getting out the truck he looked and couldn't see anyone coming this way so maybe he had time to warn someone what they were doing. As he stopped a moment to determine where he would go to call for help he heard a large blast.

Missy's shot was right on target hitting William in the back side which would never have caused his death if he hadn't been carrying a stick of dynamite in his back pocket. The bird shot pierced his back pocket striking the dynamite which immediately exploded which caused the dynamite in Randy's back pocket to explode as well. The two explosions were deadly enough by themselves but there was the matter of the gas grill tanks which were ignited by the two explosions. Sailing into the air they finally fell to earth like bombs in a war zone. One landed on the roof of the barn tearing through into the hay loft starting a fire. Another landed in the pen next to the barn where Myron was which would had been alright if not for hitting Myron on the head just as he was about to mount a lady friend of his. The others fell aimlessly around the farm.

Watching in shock at the destruction Joseph didn't know whether to stay still or run. Finally, he decided the best thing for him was to head home, his Father wouldn't be coming back.

Missy stood up and watched as the house was completely destroyed in a matter of seconds. There was nothing left, the house was gone except for the safe that sat exactly where it always sat. Looking behind her Missy realized the barn was on fire so she ran and got her horse and stood there in with tears falling down her cheeks as the neighbors and fire trucks and ambulances pulled in the drive. She wanted to move but for some reason she couldn't, all she could do was look where the house had once stood and cry holding her horse.

As she stood there with tears streaming down her face she saw Arnold and Rachel speeding down the drive. Arnold got out the car and as he ran by Missy she started to say, "It was awful..,' but before she could say anything else he ran by her not stopping or looking at her. He stood for a moment looking at what was left of his house and the barn when he looked toward the pen and saw Myron on his side. Arnold ran to the fence and climbed over, rushing to his side he began to cry as he stooped down to touch him. He stood there crying as he looked at Myron who apparently had been able to get it up one last time just before his demise.

Rachel got out of the car and watched Arnold crying over Myron and then noticed a tin box lying next to the drive. She walked over and picked it up and carried it over to Missy. "Missy here you take this. Make good use of it."

Wiping away the tears Missy asked, "What is this?'

"Over the years I have taken money out your Father's billfold every night and put it in this tin box. I don't need the money. I just did it because I could. Maybe I thought I would get his attention one day, but I never did."

"You don't want it?"

"No, I am going back to where I came from. I'll never be back to this place again. I wish I could have been a better Mother but I wasn't. You need to go ahead and graduate early and get down to Nashville to get ready for next year. Use the money to get you a good place to stay. Maybe you will be able to forgive me some day."

Rachel walked over to her car and backed out past the fire trucks and headed down the road. Later in the year Arnold and Rachel were officially divorced. She never got any of his money, nor did she ever want any of it.

Wendell Manchester was handling the investigation at the Richman farm since Sheriff Montgomery couldn't be located. The sheriff had slipped over to Covington to the east to see Rose Samuels. Rose was a 42 year old woman with a shapely body with dark red hair and a desire to please whoever she was with at the time. Rose had been arrested by a State Policeman as a part of an uncover operation for selling Fentanyl, Methadone, and Oxycodone on the square. Rose's friend at the time was a druggist's assistant who realized people didn't count how many pills were in the bottles of drugs. So she started shorting them just a little so she could sell them to Rose who found buyers on the street. On Saturday nights Rose would sit by her car on the town square and talk to the locals. Finally, the buyers showed up and she made a handsome profit. The problem for Rose was one of the buyers was an uncover policeman so later that month they arrested her and hauled her off to the jail.

They figured once Rose was in jail she would tell all but she refused to tell them anything. The reality was she didn't have much to tell except for Lucy at the drug store but they didn't know that so they kept asking her to spill what she knew for a deal. Realizing everyone thought she was part of bigger ring of dealers one evening she asked the Sheriff to have a private conversation. Sheriff Montgomery figured breaking the case would insure his reelection so he agreed to talk with her. As the Sheriff took her into the interrogation room she asked that the monitor be turned off and that everything said be private, "Because I am afraid for my life."

The Sheriff looked at her and decided this was his big chance to one up the State Police so he turned off the monitors. As he sat down Rose slowly got down on her knees before him and before he could object she was fast at work at making the Sheriff a happy man. From that night on the Sheriff would work late hours questioning Rose privately. One evening Rose mentioned she was afraid of going to prison, "Is there anything you could do to help me? I would really enjoy having you over at my place in Covington. We could have some real fun and not have to worry about getting caught. You know I would be very very grateful."

The sheriff looked into her eyes as she bent forward over him and managed to whisper, "I'll see what I can do," as she began to pleasure him.

Three days later the State police came to get the evidence for the trial and realized it was missing along with the video evidence. The prosecutor was furious and demanded to know what happened but no one could figure how it happened so Rose was released. Since that day each week the Sheriff made his way over to Covington to enjoy the fruits of his deception.

Deputy Wendell Manchester loved being in charge and didn't bother with much of an effort to locate the Sheriff. Ordering people around made him feel important and he felt if he did a good job he would have a real chance to get the job of his dreams, a State policeman. After he interviewed everyone he told Zeke, a deputy that had been on the force only a year, to go pick up Joseph and bring him to the station. Zeke looked at Wendell and paused, "Why am I picking him up?"

"First because I told you to and second because people saw him running down the road."

Zeke got into his car and made his way to Joe's trailer where he saw Joe waiting on the steps. Walking up to Joe, "They want me to take you down to the jail."

Joseph got up and began walking to the car, "I figured they would be coming for me. I just didn't figure it would be you."

"I wish it weren't me. We were good friends in school. I hate this."

"You are just doing what is right."

As they sat in the car Zeke handed Joe some cuffs, "Look when we get to jail put those on. They will expect me to have you cuffed. And one other thing, don't tell them anything. Just ask for a lawyer."

Arriving at the station Joe put the cuffs on and walked into the jail. Wendell was there with a frown on his face seeing how Joe was cuffed, "Hey Zeke he should be cuffed with his hands behind his back. When are you going to learn? Put him in the interrogation room."

As Zeke walked by Wendell said, "Go get me a couple burgers from Morgan's Diner."

"Are you going to feed Joe?"

"No, I am going to eat something and let him wait. He needs to suffer a while."

As Zeke walked off he looked back, "Get your own food, I don't work for you."

An hour later after Wendell got back from the diner he walked into the interrogation room and asked Joe, "Are you ready to tell me what you did?"

"Sure, I was ready an hour ago." It was like opening a drink upside down everything flowed out of Joe barely giving Wendell a moment to get a word in. He told how his Father had stolen cars and sold them to Billy Ryan and had traded for the truck he drove his Father and Randy. Randy had stolen the dynamite and what his Father was trying to steal from Arnold Richman. Sitting there hearing the name Billy Ryan Wendell's eyes lit up. Finally he had evidence against that fool. He had known for a long time Billy was up to no good, he just never could get the evidence, now he had it.

Walking out of the interrogation room he turned to Mick and announced he was headed to Billy Ryan's place to arrest him. Mick was shocked to hear Billy Ryan mentioned, "Don't you think you should wait for the Sheriff? He will be mighty mad with you going off arresting people without running it by him."

"The Sheriff isn't here. I am in charge and I'm going to arrest that crooked fool. I will need back up so you and Louis drive down there."

So Wendell went blazing down the highway with his sirens roaring with Louis and Mick following. As they made their way down the country gravel roads the dust flew up in the air forming a red cloud from the lights on the cars. It was of course a smoke signal for Billy as he looked out the front door of his house. Walking back in he told his wife to get the suitcases ready and then he picked up the phone and dialed saying as the other side picked up, "It's time." Hanging the phone up he yelled, "Hurry we need to be out in front of the house."

Billy and his wife walked out in front of the barn with their hands up waiting on Wendell. Wendell's car skidded to a stop throwing rocks and dust as he jumped out. Rushing over to Billy he quickly patted him down and cuffed him and then did the same to his wife.

Billy waited until Wendell was done and asked, "Do you mind telling me what this is all about."

"You are dealing in stolen cars. Looking back at Mick he said put them in my car."

Wendell walked into the barn to Billy's office and began to go through the file cabinet. Louis walked in seeing Wendell going through the files and asked, "Don't you need a search warrant for that?"

"I'm not waking the judge. I'll get one in the morning."

"I don't think it works that way."

"No wonder you are still a deputy after twenty years. You have to take chances from time to time. Look at this, get me a glass." Wendell held up a bottle of scotch he found in the file cabinet.

Louis just walked away shaking his head wondering, 'How long will I have to put up with that fool?'

The Sheriff satisfied and refreshed got in his car to head back to Springtown when heard several voices over the radio. Checking in with dispatch he was brought up to speed on all that had happened while he was out of town engaged in his dalliance. He immediately pressed the accelerator and went down the road with the siren blaring and lights flashing as he made his way to Billy's place.

Getting out of the car he went to Wendell's car where Billy and his wife sat handcuffed. Getting in the front he looked back at Billy, "What is going on?"

"Wendell says he has evidence. I trust you remember what we paid for all these years?"

"Yes, yes Billy I remember. Just give me some time to work this out."

Getting out of the car he yelled at Louis, Get them out of the car and take the cuffs off of them."

Walking into the barn office he saw Wendell drinking scotch and going through the files. "You don't have a warrant to do that."

"Now all of a sudden we are going to have search warrants? It never stopped you before."

Walking back outside the sweat was forming on his brow as he tried to think of how he could get out of this mess. Suddenly down lane came three black Ford Expeditions in a cloud of dust slamming to a stop. Out of the first vehicle a man in a black suit and tie walked up to the Sheriff pulling out his badge as he said, "FBI, we need to take this case over. Please stand aside and let us do our work."

Wendell walked out of the barn with the scotch and yelled, "You ain't takin' this case over."

The sheriff thought a moment if the FBI gets into this they will know what arrangement he had with Billy and that will result in him going to federal prison. "No this is our case we aren't letting you take it over."

The FBI agent with the badge looked at the Sheriff and with a smile asked him to walk over to a tree so they could talk privately. As they reached the tree the agent pulled out his phone and began to show the Sheriff several photos of him taking cash from Randy. After showing him the photos he looked at the Sheriff, "Randy is a valuable asset and we need to protect him. Now if you will go your way we will forget about these photos and take over this case. But, you don't I will have to show these to the US Attorney."

The Sheriff gulped and simply said, "Very well you take it over." Walking back toward the barn he yelled at Louis to turn Randy and his wife over to the FBI. Walking into the barn he said this is a federal case so they are taking over. Wendell looked up, "No, they aren't taking this case."

The Sheriff looked at Wendell and shrugged his shoulders, "If you want a recommendation from me for that State police job you will get your ass out of there and let the Feds do their work."

Wendell and the rest drove away turning Randy and his wife over to the Feds. The agent in charge looked at Randy and said, "Are you packed?"

"Yes, we have our suitcases ready to go."

"Ok, we are going to relocate you. This will be the end of our relationship. We will give you a new identity and a place to live but if you do any misdeeds in the future you will be on your own. Do you understand?"

"Yes, perfectly."

So ended the years of uncover work Billy had done helping the government to crack down on drug smugglers from Costa Rica. Billy had helped the smugglers in the early days hiding drugs in special compartments he built in the vehicles. Having got caught along the way he decided helping the Feds was better than spending time in prison, so the last several years a small time junk yard was a major part of an international drug ring which several months later lead to 35 Federal Warrants for drug dealers stretching from Costa Rica, Mexico, Texas and Louisianna.

Billy and his wife ended up in a small town in Vermont with a few dollars and a car furnished by the government. Billy was no fool he knew the day would come he would be whisked off to some distant place with a new identity with a few dollars from the government, so he had started a rainy day fund. His rainy day fund was kept in cash in the liner of their suitcases. So when Billy arrived in Vermont he arrived a wealthy man and never worked another day spending most days driving around the countryside with his wife in a red 1959 Austin Healey. The tattoos that adorned his neck and arms were not permanent, so once he got to Vermont he washed them away and began the life of a respectable Vermont citizen.

Back at the jail Wendell confronted the Sheriff, "Why did you let them take the case? They always push us aside. Why are you so weak?"

"Look Wendell just shut up. If you say anything else I am going to fire your ass."

"You don't have the guts to fire me."

The Sheriff exhaled, "You are fired you dumb son of a bitch."

Wendell didn't get the job with the State police but he did run against the Sheriff in the next election. The Sheriff had the backing of Arnold Richman so he won in a landslide. Wendell took a job at Wal-Mart as a security officer.

CHAPTER FIVE

The night of the explosion Arnold opened the safe and pulled out one hundred dollars. Looking at the Deputy Sheriff, "They surely weren't breaking in to steal money. I never have more than this in the safe. They were probably after the grill tanks."

"Well maybe they figured you have a lot of money in here from the grain."

"All that money is direct deposited these days and even if they gave me cash I wouldn't keep it here. It was the gas tanks they were after."

Arnold mourned the lost of his bull, barn, house, and wife in that order. Actually losing Rachel turned out to be a good thing. He was a great catch for the ladies in a three county area, he had money, his teeth, and a waste line that didn't extend much over his belt. As a result the women were bringing him their sympathy and loving arms to console.

Once the shock of the explosion was over Arnold began to prepare for the future which meant a new barn and house. While the house was being built he had two RVS brought for him and Missy to live in. He didn't want to live in close proximity to Missy so he had the additional RV brought for her. As the days turned into weeks the women without a man began bringing food to his door. They would show up asking if he was doing ok since Rachel left and thought he might like a cobbler pie or fried chicken or cream pie. Although they were there to console him they refused to go the extra mile to complete the sale.

Jenny Logan a 43 year old divorcee that was the lead singer in the Jesus Supreme quartet was willing to go the extra mile. She went to Arnold's church but most Sundays her and the quartet were singing at churches throughout Southern Indiana. Jenny had long blonde hair that fell down to her shoulders and looked as soft as cotton with a figure that always caught the attention of the men where they sang. Jenny got the news of Arnold's misfortune while singing at a church social in Cedarville and knew immediately what she was going to do.

Each Thursday Jenny showed up at Arnold's place with a T-Bone steak which she prepared and then when he was rested she gave him desert. She knew food was important but serving herself up as the desert was what she felt would close the deal and hook Arnold. What she didn't understand was Arnold was like most men greedy and unable to look beyond the moment of satisfaction. He didn't realize Jenny was fishing and the bait was her and he was the fish. So, after eight weeks of steak and her for desert Jenny decided it was time for her next move, she just quit going to Arnold's on Thursday.

Arnold was annoyed at first but as one week lead into three he realized he wanted Jenny, so he got in his truck and drove over to her place. Walking up to the door he was certain she would see him and want him as much as he wanted her. Opening the door Jenny smiled knowing she was winning. Arnold stepped forward, "Jenny I have missed. Won't you come over to my place again."

Jenny looked down and paused for effect, "Not sure that is a good idea. I have been talking to Leo Barnes and he wants to date me."

"That used car dealer. Hell he is nothing but a skirt chaser."

"Don't speak unkindly of a fellow Christian."

"Jenny I love you. I want you in my life."

Jenny realized she had the hook solidly in Arnold, now it was just a matter of getting him in the boat, "I fell for you and let you do things I should never have down outside of marriage. I am ashamed and I just can't go on that way. The only way I will be with a man is if he is my husband."

"Arnold fell to his knees, "Jenny please marry me."

Jenny smiled and said, "Yes darling I will marry you." As she embraced Arnold she realized she had landed the big fish.

Jenny and Arnold were married at a small ceremony two weeks later because Arnold was desperate for desert. Arnold lived in the RV until the new house was built and then rebuilt to meet Jenny's demands. First was the great room needed to have a stone fireplace with hardwood floors and a large marble mantel and the deck needed to be larger so they could have friends over for a cookout and sit while she and her quartet sang. She also needed a room in the basement that was soundproof so she could record her music. Arnold realized three months after their marriage his need for desert was costing him a whole lot of money.

Missy wasn't around to see the newlyweds having left in February to Nashville. She found a nice apartment close to the Belmont Campus and began a new chapter in her life. A chapter without Rachel or Arnold, a chapter free from them. Several weeks after getting her apartment settled she walked pass the mirror in the bedroom and noticed something unusual about herself, she was smiling.

CHAPTER SIX

Judge Stevens, Sheriff Montgomery, and the prosecutor for the county, Jerrod Stone met with Arnold at the Judge's fishing cabin close to the Blue River. As they sat down around the table the Judge passed beers out and began by saying, "I think everyone here knows this meeting never happened. If word got out about this we all would be in big trouble. Does everyone agree this must be kept secret?"

Looking around the room the Judge saw each face acknowledge the meeting had to be secret. There was silence for a moment as if everyone was afraid to say anything. Finally, Arnold broke the silence, "So what do you want from me?"

The prosecutor straightened in his chair, "We want to know what you want? I think the evidence shows Joseph was actually tied up and forced in the truck, so I think we should let him go without any charges."

"My house and barn was destroyed. My prize million dollar bull killed and you want the son of one of the gang let go?"

The Judge stepped forward, "Look Arnold the evidence is unclear but there were rope burns on Joseph's wrists and there was skin torn by the tape. So his story seems to fit the physical evidence."

The sheriff saw a chance to gain favor with Arnold, "It was the perfect alibi. He did it to make it appear that he was not involved. And all of you are falling for it."

Arnold looked at the Sheriff with a smile, "Exactly, he hid these things to himself. Why would he be running down the road otherwise?"

Prosecutor Stone finally interjected, "Ok, so the answer is you want us to prosecute Joseph to the full extent of the law, right?"

"Yes, I worked hard to get each of you elected and I would expect you standing by me in this difficult time."

The Judge as was his normal way said, "Oh it is decided Joseph will be charged as a conspirator and move forward to trial. How about some whiskey now?"

They sat there the rest of the evening laughing and drinking. Finally after several whiskeys and beers the Sheriff called his men to drive everyone home. Once again Arnold was getting what Arnold wanted.

Joseph was brought into court the next Tuesday and after some legal details told the Judge he didn't have any money to hire a lawyer. Judge Stevens tried not to smile as the assigned the case the public defender, Morton Sinclair. The Judge knew this would please Arnold since Morton was simply inept.

Morton Sinclair was just out of law school having passed the bar six months ago. He had planned to fight for social justice in a country of systemic racism. His focus as a law student was the fight for equal justice for the down trodden in a country of great wealth. His Father, the president of the Covington Bank and Loan, thought his son was a foolish young man that would give up his silly ideas once the real world hit him in the face.

Morton applied to several groups that were fighting the good fight as he said but they were not interested in a young white boy. They wanted to diversify the legal team and Morton was not diverse. So Morton came home to Covington to the family basement and waited until someone needed to fight for justice. The problem was after three months no one had needed his assistance in the fight for justice and his Father was restless with his son doing nothing but spending his days on Instagram complaining about the greed of a capitalist society. So his father walked into his room in the basement and announced that Carter City to the East needed a public defender and he was taking the job. Morton complained, "I don't want to be a part of the system of oppression."

His Father laughed, "You are either going to take the job or you are going to be a part of the system of homelessness."

Morton chose the job. He was of course the best possible choice for the job according to the prosecutor since he knew absolutely nothing about criminal law except it was evil and oppressive. The judge was also happy with Morton a young dumb public defender could be knocked around and wouldn't fight back. The criminal lawyers in the county and surrounding areas were overjoyed since it meant anyone with anything would sell it to pay their bills rather than have Morton appointed to represent them. They sold cars, rings, and a good deal of dope to avoid having Morton as their lawyer.

Morton often found ways to include his fight against systemic racism in his closing arguments for his clients. The fact none of them were black never seem to matter to him, he had a cause and he was determined to fight the good fight even if it was in a county of white people.

As far as Morton knew he was the best thing that the criminal justice system had seen since Clarence Darrow. However, unlike Clarence Darrow he hadn't won a case yet, but as he often said, "It is early in my career."

The prosecutor spent the last three nights unable to sleep afraid Joseph would hire some high priced defense lawyer. He knew his political career depended upon keeping Arnold happy and losing the case would not make Arnold happy. The holes in his case were huge and a good defense lawyer could drive a semi through on the way to a victory. He just didn't want to have to go back into private practice again, it was too difficult fighting over the crumbs left behind by the high powered law firms.

Sitting in court the prosecutor almost cried tears of joy when Joseph told the Judge he didn't have the money to hire his own attorney. The judge exhaled as well. Now he wouldn't have Arnold on his back complaining the boy got off after destroying his life. Now justice would appear to be done and everyone but Joseph would be happy and the prosecutor and Judge wouldn't have their careers cut short. Turning to Joseph the Judge said, "I will appoint Morton Sinclair, our capable public defender to represent you." The prosecutor couldn't help but wonder how the Judge said that without laughing.

Two days later Myron went to the jail to consult with Joseph. Sitting down across from Myron he asked, "What you need to know is I am innocent. I didn't do it."

Myron sat back in his chair trying to look the part of defense attorney, "Well you need to know they have a good deal of evidence that says you were involved. You were running away from the scene. They have witnesses saying they saw you come home that evening just before William and Randy showed up."

"Well if they saw them then surely they saw them take me out to the truck tied up and throwing me in the back."

"There is nothing in their statements about any of that. I am sure if they had it would be in there."

"Well I didn't do it."

"There is an offer on the table. They will agree to six years in prison for a plea of guilty."

"I didn't do it. I'm not pleading to anything."

Myron got up to leave and as he walked to the door he turned to Joseph, "Think about it. You could end up with 20 years if you go to trial."

Joseph just sat there shaking his head, "I know everyone in here says they are innocent but I am. I am not going to plead guilty."

Myron shrugged his shoulders not knowing what to say. He was desperate to get Joseph to plead since he was fearful of a trial, after all it would be his first. Finally Myron said, "Look, think about the plea deal. I'll be back in a few days to check on things."

They took Joseph back to his cell. The sheriff had him placed in a cell by himself down a long hall way. He figured the isolation would break him down and bring him around to taking a plea. The sheriff was wrong, Joseph enjoyed being alone.

Each day a deputy brought a small cart of books around for the prisoners to choose from. They were books given to the jail by churches. Most of the books were either Bibles or Christian related except for a couple. Looking at the books on the cart Joseph noticed one that was different with a blue and white cover entitled, 'Did You Ever See A Dreaming Walking.' Pointing to it Joseph asked to have it to read. Sitting down on his bunk he opened it and began trying to read. Instantly he was mesmerized by words used by William Buckley in the introduction. There was something about his prose that attracted him even if he didn't fully understand what he was saying. Diving into the book he continued to be amazed and drawn to it. It was a book on Conservative Thought in the 20th century containing works from several authors. Reading through the book he was drawn to the words and logic and became desirous of being able to express himself in the same manner. At that moment he wasn't sure he agreed or fully understood what he was reading but he knew he wanted to be able to understand it and express his thoughts in the same way.

It is common for an inmate to have a conversion but most of time it is a 'Come to Jesus' moment not a conservative conversion. For Joseph it wasn't a conversion to Conservative Thought, it was a conversion to thinking. For years he had lived life as if there was nothing beyond the moment. Now he was beginning to see it differently, now he saw a world of knowledge and he wanted to take it all in. His political views would be molded later as he sought knowledge in a world of books he never knew existed.

Each day he begged for more books along with a dictionary to understand the words he was reading. The guard brought a bag of books the library was tossing. The books were torn and worn but Joseph treated them carefully making his way through. Along the way he read, 'The Myth of Sisyphus' by Albert Camus, 'Man's Search for meaning' by Victor Frankl, 'Pilgrim's Progress' by John Bunyan, 'Animal Farm', '1984' and "Road to Homage' by George Orwell, and 'Brave New World' by Aldous Huxley. Now, after opening his mind to different ideas and thinkers he was a convert to Conservative Thought.

Joseph continued consumed with desire for more and more books as the weeks wore on with no end in sight. Myron afraid of a trial had asked for continuations so he could prepare, but the reality was it was because of his fear and hope the wait would wear Joseph down.

Myron walked into the room set aside for lawyers to talk with their clients and looked at Joseph, "Well the judge won't give me another continuance so we are going to trial in three weeks. So this is serious. If you plead guilty they will agree to a five year sentence. That means with good behavior and time served you would be out in two years. That is a good deal. You have to take it or else we go to trial and you end up getting twenty years. So, what do you say?"

"I didn't do it. I am not going to plead guilty to something I didn't do."

"Don't do this to me. Don't make me go to trial. You have to plead."

"Nope, sorry but I am not guilty so you better get ready for trial."

Myron didn't say anything as he grabbed his papers and stormed out of the room. He now knew he faced humiliation at the hands of the prosecutor. 'Maybe I could withdraw. I could say I am sick or something or I have a conflict.'

Joseph watched as Myron stormed out of the room and began to get up to go to his cell when the guard stepped in, "Sit back down you have two more visitors."

'Two more visitors? I haven't had any all this time and now I have two?'

Sitting wondering who could be coming to see him the door opened and missy walked in sitting down across from him. Joseph couldn't help but smile seeing Missy, "Oh my I am so glad to see you. I have wondered how you were."

Missy stiffened her back and raised up in her chair, "I graduated from high school in the middle of the year so I could go on to Nashville to get ready for next fall's classes. I have wondered every night one thing, were you in on this? I won't tell anyone what you say, but I need to know. I need to have some peace of mind."

"Oh Missy, no. That night my Father and Randy came in the trailer and began to brag about what they were going to do and I said they couldn't do that because of you. They were afraid I would tell so they tied me up and threw me in the bed of the truck. I promise I would never have been a part of this ever. The police saw the rope burns on my arms and ankles and the torn skin around my lips. I don't care what happens to me but I care more than anything that you know I did not take part in this."

As Missy heard joseph she began to cry. The tears flowed down her face as she looked up at him, "I knew you would never do anything like this. I just knew it, but there was a part of me that doubted you. Please forgive me. I should have been a better friend."

"Better friend? You are the best friend a person could have."

"Thank you. I love you friend. Is there anything I can do for you?"

"I love you. You could get me a book. I really would like to read 'Crime and Punishment.' Also, could you find a way to get my cell phone? I thought I managed to turn it on to record them. Myron can't seem to get it and they won't let me have it."

"Sure I will get to work on it. Write down your password so I can open it if I can't get out of the evidence locker. I have to go now, but I will be back. Wait you haven't said anything about how I look."

"You look beautiful as always."

"I have lost a hundred pounds. You didn't notice?"

"Yes I noticed. But you don't understand, you have always been beautiful to me. Now you are thinner and beautiful."

Missy knew she wasn't supposed to touch him but nevertheless she leaned over and kissed him on the forehead and walked out of the room.

CHAPTER SEVEN

Zeke Taylor a sheriff's deputy for the past year was Joseph's only friend in school other than Missy. Missy went to his house that afternoon asking if he could get Joseph's phone out of the evidence locker. Zeke knew it was too dangerous to remove it since the new security cameras had been put in place after Rose's Samuels evidence came up missing.

Thinking for a moment finally he offered, "Look the security camera is positioned to see anything anyone takes out of the room.

You can look at evidence inside and they won't know. Sunday night it is dead around there, I can go in and pull the evidence locker out and open it to see what is on it."

"That would be great. Thanks, call me Sunday night."

Sunday night it was a normal slow night with Ruth sitting at the console monitoring calls and Cecil, a 75 year old jailer, sitting in a chair at the end of the hall to the cells half asleep. Walking in Zeke looked at Ruth, "Hey, I am working a little on a case and need to see the evidence again."

"Ok but remember the cameras will catch you if you take anything out of there. So don't do anything stupid."

"Sure thing." Zeke made his way down the hall past Cecil and into the evidence room putting in the code to gain entrance. Looking at the index on the wall he saw Joseph's evidence was in lockers six, seven, and eight. Going to the lockers he read the index outside the drawer to see what was inside. The phone was in locker eight. As he looked at the index he noted three notes below the where is said phone. The notes said the phone had been removed to obtain data from it on three occasions. The final note stated the phone data was opened and the information was contained in the locker in the form of a transcript. Opening the locker Zeke thumbed through the evidence until he came to the transcript of information on the phone. The transcript contained text messages over the past year which were personal and then he saw the transcript of the night of the crime. Looking down at the transcript his body began to shake as he saw what was contained on the phone recording. Quickly he took his phone out and took several photos of the transcript and shoved it back in the locker.

Hurrying down the hall he met the sheriff, "So Ruth called me and said you were in the evidence locker?"

"Yes, I wanted to check some evidence on the Comstock case."

"That is a stupid disorderly and public intoxication case. Why would you be checking it."

"I'm new at this and I wanted to make sure my testimony tomorrow was correct."

"Boy you are sure green. Get out of here and quit coming in after hours."

As soon as Zeke got into his car he sent the information to Missy who was staying at the Covington Motor lodge. Looking at the photos Missy shook with anger and joy knowing what she had in her hands. As Zeke drove home he realized he was going to have to find a better place to work. He thought, 'I guess I will take them up on that offer from the Covington city police.'

The next day Missy made her way to the farm. Seeing Arnold feeding the pigs in the lot next to the barn made her skin crawl. Walking over to the fence she yelled, "you better come over here I have some things to go over with you."

Walking to the fence Arnold had a big smile as he approached Missy, "Wow you have lost a ton of weight. You look great."

"Shup up. I don't want to hear from you about my weight. I am here about Joseph. You know he didn't do it and you need to tell your peons to drop the charges."

"Missy, I can't make them do anything. After all the evidence sure shows he did do it."

"You are a liar."

"I am not going to have my daughter talk to me that way."

"Look if you want me to talk to you differently then don't lie to me. If Joseph goes to trial I am going to take the witness stand for him. I will tell everyone you paid the claims adjuster a kick back and he paid you for Myron as if he were in the prime of his life."

"How did you know that?"

"I didn't. I just know how you operate and figured that was what you did," Missy laughed, than going on, "I will testify you see Rose Samuels every Wednesday. I know that because I followed you a few times. I will testify you paid for Jenny Morgan's abortion because you had knocked her up. I know that because she told me. Oh by the way she was 16 when you knocked her up. Then I will show the jury the transcript from Joseph's phone of the night of the crime. It clearly shows he had a gun to his head and was tied up and that everyone knew it."

"I can't believe my own daughter would turn against me."

"Believe what you want but you have twenty four hours to get the charges dropped or I take this to Myron."

Missy walked away from her Father with a smile on her face knowing she was free of him. She was on her own and life was hers free of him. She could smile now.

Sitting at the table Joseph wondered who the second visitor was. As he sat there he watched as Reverend Logan of the Mill Baptist Church walked through the door. 'What in the world could he want with me,' Joseph asked himself.

Sitting down the Reverend asked, "How are you son?"

"I am doing fine sir."

"Well let me get to the reason I am here. My church has a deal with the landlord for the trailers where you live to clean out the ones that are left unattended. We clean them and remove everything throwing away the trash. I always go along to make sure we don't throw away anything personal or of value. Any of those things we put in a tub and keep it the basement. We leave it there in case the family wants any of the items."

"That is nice of you."

"Thanks. Well we cleaned out your trailer and I found a shoe box under the bed with some pictures and papers, so I set them aside to keep."

"Thanks I appreciate that."

"In the box were four pieces of paper that appeared to be shares of stock. I took them to a lawyer who checked them out several times. He found out they were real. They are four shares of stock for $250 each or a total of one thousand."

Joseph smiled, "Yes my Mother loved to tell me the story of how my Father did some work for people in California and they paid him

$1000 in cash and the four pieces of paper. She always laughed when she told the story.”

“Well those pieces of paper are stock certificates for Apple Stock. They are worth about nine million dollars today.”

Joseph sat back in his chair and just looked at the Reverend trying to make sense of what he had just heard. His mind kept saying, ‘This kind of thing doesn’t happen to me. This doesn’t happen to a Samuels. There has to be catch in all of this.’ Finally, he leaned forward, “Ok so why aren’t they any good now?”

“They are good. They are properly registered stock certificates and they are in your name.”

“Yes, after your brother Randy died your Father signed them over to you. Didn’t he tell you?”

“No, we never had much to say to each other. I guess it is the one good thing he did for me.”

“I put them in a safety box at the bank in Covington. I have the key and will keep it at the church until you get out, if that is ok with you?”

“Yes, yes that is great. Please do. Thank you.”

PART TWO

CHAPTER ONE

Judge Stevens looked down from the bench and asked, "Mr. Prosecutor you have informed the court you have a motion to make. Please present your motion."

"Your honor recently the State learned of new evidence that points to the innocence of the defendant. As a result we move to dismiss all charges against Joseph Samuels."

"The court grants the motion of the State dismissing all charges against Joseph Samuels and orders his immediate release."

Myron looked in shock at Joseph and finally stammered, "We won. I won, my first victory."

Joseph looked at him and laughed, "Yes you won."

The prosecutor walked back to his office and as he entered the door he saw Missy sitting in the waiting room. "What are you here for?"

"I am here to talk to you privately."

"Sure come in and have a seat."

Missy walked in but remained standing as the prosecutor sat down in his red leather wing back chair. Once he settled in his chair, Missy began, "By now you know what evidence I have. I am giving you a chance to resign by Friday or I will send what I know to the Bar Association, your choice."

The prosecutor stood up as Missy started to leave, "Look can we talk about this."

Missy looked back as she shut the door laughing.

The prosecutor handed in his resignation Friday at 3:00 pm stating he needed to attend to family matters.

Later the same day Missy went to the Sheriff and sat across his desk as he fidgeted with a pencil. She waited a few moments to allow the silence to get to him and then finally she said, "You will need to resign just like the prosecutor. I am sure he has told you what I have."

A smile formed on the Sherriff's face as he spoke, "Look little girl I had nothing to do with any of that. None of that can be pinned on me. So you can just take yourself back to Nashville. I ain't resigning."

Missy sat in silence for a moment and then proceeded, "Sheriff my Father has been screwing Rose Samuels for a long time. During that time I followed him over there to see what he was up to. One day recently I went to Rose and asked her about my Father. You know she told me on tape she was getting it on with my Father and you. Now the interesting part is she said she had to give it up to you because you destroyed the evidence against her. Oh and she has you talking about it on her phone. Now isn't that delicious. So do you want to resign or do you want me to go to the US Attorney."

The sheriff tried hard to keep from showing his anger but finally he couldn't help it, "You damn bitches know it all."

"Now no reason to get personal here. You have until Friday to resign or I go to the US Attorney. Understand? Oh and Rose says there is no need for you to come over there anymore."

Friday at 4:15pm the Sheriff announced he was resigning. Missy left the judge alone, since he had given her Mother some pleasure over the years. She did stop by his office that same day telling him if it wasn't for her Mother she would have him resign. He looked at her and began to cry. Missy walked away saying, "Your tears mean nothing to me."

Missy asked Zeke to bring Joseph to the Travel Lodge Bar after he got his things. As he walked into the bar Missy ran to him and hugged him as tears ran down her face. Zeke stood back with tears in his eyes as Joseph kept trying to talk through his tears. Finally he said, "Beautiful I have never known anyone as strong and pretty as you. Thanks for saving my life."

Missy looked up, "Well thank Zeke also. He put everything on the line to get the transcript."

Joseph looked back at his old friend and reached out to him. They all stood there in a hug with tears falling. Finally, Missy said, "I know you don't have any money so I got you a room here for a couple months."

"Funny story, you see I may have some money in a few days." He proceeded to tell them of his good fortune. Promising he would repay Missy he thanked her for the loan of money.

"I have several things to take care of here but when I am finished I will be down to Nashville to take you out on a real date, if you will go," Joseph said with a questioning look.

"Yes I will go out with you. Just hurry down there soon."

CHAPTER TWO

Joseph went to the church and got the safe deposit box key and retrieved the stock certificates. Going to a money manager to handle his investment he decided to cash out a million dollars of the stocks leaving the rest alone. He then took a check to the Reverend for $50,000 for the church.

Then Zeke and him drove a new Cambry with all the options and leather seats over to the Covington diner. Walking in the door Joseph approached the young waitress, "You don't know me but I was in here a long time ago and heard how you had lost your car."

"Yes that is true. Someone stole it."

"Well my Father stole it. I found out about it and I wanted to make it right. So I bought that Cambry outside for you. I hope you like it. Here are the keys and title."

"Oh my, are you serious?"

"Yes, my Father was a thief and he got blown up a while back and I came into some money. I wanted to get this car for you."

"Thank you, thank you, thank you."

"Come on out and check it out," Joseph said as he walked away.

Walking away from the waitress as she sat behind the wheel Joseph felt he had finally done something good in his life. It was a good feeling, he smiled at Zeke, "Let's get back to the motel."

As they made their way to the motel Joseph turned to Zeke, "What are you going to do now? Are you going to stay with the Sheriff's office?"

"No, there is no way I can stay there. I am trying to get on with the Covington Police Department."

"Is that what you want to do the rest of your life."

"My dream is to start a security business. The banks all want a professional group for security as well as the grain elevators and other industries in the area. There isn't anyone qualified to provide the service so there are these untrained people working as security right and that creates a good deal of liability for them."

"Why don't you start the business now?"

"It takes money to get started and I need to save up over the next few years so I can get it going."

"Start now. I will invest in your business. I will take a ten percent interest in the business."

"Are you serious? You don't have to do that.'

"I know I don't have to but I want to. Hell, you saved me by taking a big chance. Plus it is business, I get ten percent of the business."

"Wow that is great. Let me show you the office I want to rent for the business."

"So you have done some serious dreaming?

"Yes every day I revise my plans and dream."

"Well partner let's see the office."

Two days later Joseph packed up what he had and got into his new truck. It was new to him but was actually ten years old. He went to buy a new one but just felt he was wasting money so he bought a blue Ford 150 with 110,000 miles. He told himself, 'Maybe later I will feel comfortable buying myself that new truck, but not now.'

Joseph drove to Nashville and checked in at the Comfort Inn in the Green Hills area and as he put his bag of clothes down he called Missy. "Hey how are you, it's me. I am here in Nashville finally. I thought maybe we could go out this evening for dinner. What do you think?"

"That sounds good but I just can't tonight. I have to study. Why don't you meet me at the Frothy Monkey on 12th Street South. You know where that is?"

"No, but I will get directions. What time?"

"In an hour."

Hanging up the phone Joseph sat on the bed thinking there was something about her voice that told him things had changed. He kept trying to convince himself it was just his imagination but still the doubts continued. He opened the small case in his hand and took out the ring. He had bought it for Missy. He knew it was too soon to marry but he wanted her to know he wanted to marry her and be her fiancé. He wanted to start the future with her in his life.

Joseph got to the coffee shop thirty minutes early excited to see her. Sitting in the back room at a long table he waited. She finally came in twenty minutes late. As she walked toward him he got up and hugged her and in that moment he was sure something had changed. She hugged him but it was not the same, things had changed. He wondered, 'Have I done something? What could I have done that changed things?'

Sitting down Missy took a sip of her coffee and looked up, "It is great to see you Joseph. How are you doing?"

"I am doing great. I really am happy to see you."

Missy looked down at her cup and fondled it as if she was trying to gather herself, finally she looked up, "There is something I need to tell you. I have started dating someone."

"Oh, that is why you didn't want to go out to dinner."

"Yes, please don't be angry with me. I didn't plan on becoming interested in someone but it just happened."

"Angry with you? I could never be angry with you. You have a right to have a life and do what you want. You owe me nothing. I owe you everything. I want you to be happy," as he spoke Joseph knew the words were only partially true. He wanted her to be happy but he desperately wanted her to be happy with him, but now he knew that was not to be.

"I have to go to class. Maybe we can get together again soon."

"Sure we can real soon. Take care and never forget how beautiful you are."

Joseph sat there watching as she walked away. The pit of his stomach ached as he realized they would never be. Everything he wanted was gone and he was left alone. Looking around the room he felt everyone was looking at him with sadness in her their eyes knowing he had just had his heart broken. Trying to smile Joseph walked out into the bright sun which he felt was out of place, 'There should be clouds and rain, not sun.' He walked away feeling the ring box in his pocket and the hole in his heart.

Getting back to his room he realized his plans had to be changed. He had planned to find a place in Nashville to be close to Missy, get his high school diploma and got to college, but now he needed to go someplace away from here.

As he pondered where he would go the phone rang. He quickly grabbed it thinking it might be Missy, 'Maybe she changed her mind,' he thought, but it wasn't; the voice on the line was a man.

"Hey boy this is your old Uncle Moses. How you doing?"

Moses was actually Devon Samuels, Moses was his stage name. His stage was a traveling Tent Revival where he tried saving souls and getting people to part with their money. His revivals lasted six days. The sixth day was healing day. Those who had contributed freely were offered healing prayers by the good reverend. Reverend told the folks who stood with their pocket books open begging to be healed, "Sinners you won't be healed today but the evidence of the healing will come weeks down the road if God sees your faith is strong." When someone caught him down the road another revival complaining despite all the money they had given they weren't healed, he said, "Well sinner take it up with God because of your lack of faith. I told you if you had faith you would be healed but obviously you don't."

Joseph groaned knowing why his uncle was calling, "Uncle Devon what do you want?"

"It is Moses boy. I am leading the sinners out the land of sin these days. I hear you have some money."

"I have a little."

"Well I have a way to get you a whole lot more. Invest in my ministry and we will go to the top. With some money I can book big venues and get some television time. Look boy when people come down to be healed I tell them if they have true faith they will throw their medicine on the stage. Hell, you wouldn't believe the good drugs I get. I got a fellow that buys them from me. Now if we are able to go big time we could collect a real bundle of drugs and donations. Hell we'll make money all around. What do you say boy, you want to be my partner in the fight against sin?"

"I am not going to invest in your scam."

"Boy that is hurtful. I am doing the Lord's work. I am giving you a chance to do it with me."

As Joseph hung up the phone he said, "The answer is no. I hope you enjoy hell."

Laying on the bed looking up at the ceiling he continued to think of the hole in his heart and the pain of losing Missy to another. 'If only I had got here earlier. Maybe I could get her to change her mind?' he wondered. Finally he answered his questions, 'What is done is done. I am not going to be a bother to her. I need to move on and begin living my life again. I have to let her live her life.'

As he laid there his phone rang. Again he reached for it with the faint hope it was Missy, but it wasn't.

"Nephew, this is your Aunt Rose. How are you doing?"

"How much you want?"

"Why boy that is no way to talk to your old Aunt. I just wanted to see how you were doing."

"Sorry, I am doing fine."

"I was downtown last night and a fellow had some real good dope but he wanted too much for it. I figured if I could get the money I could buy it and sell it in smaller parts and make some real money."

"I'm not giving you money to buy dope," Joseph said as he hung the phone up.

Looking at his phone and realizing the Samuels would not quit bothering him he took the battery out and threw the phone in the trash, 'I'll get a new phone in a day or two.'

The next morning Joseph got up and pointed his truck west. He had no idea where he was going he just drove. Driving looking out the window he figured he would know when he reached where he was going. At the end of day two he still hadn't seen where he wanted to stop so he continued the quest to find his home. Day three as he continued driving, he saw to the North against the bright blue sky a range of mountains. Stopping his truck he looked around, there were no houses no sign of anything other than a stream running through a valley of grass. He knew he had found his new home. He drove into Helena, Montana and said to himself, this is where I will live.

Two weeks later Joseph had a home and was going about the business of getting his high school diploma. Each night he returned to his reading. He was still reading anything William F. Buckley had written as well all the works of the Dane, Kierkegaard. He loved the way Soren wrote requiring you to wander through a mine field of words and then retrace them in an effort to understand the point being made.

Once Joseph got his high school diploma he began efforts to get admitted to Carroll College in Helena. They weren't impressed with his high school records so he had to persuade them through three interviews he was qualified before they would admit him. Before his classes were to begin and a new world was opening up to him he began to reflect on the old world he had left behind, the world of the Samuels family. He looked back and saw the circus of characters that was the Samuels and realized he wanted to break all ties with his past. He didn't want to be a Samuels any longer. After reflection he went to the offices of a local attorney and announced he wanted to change his name. He wanted his name to be Joseph Buckley from this moment forward. Six months later Joseph walked out of the courthouse no longer a Samuels he was now Joseph Buckley.

CHAPTER THREE

Leaving Joseph that day haunted Missy. She laid awake that night torn by her affection for her boyfriend and her love for Joseph. She asked herself over and over, 'Did I make a mistake? I shouldn't have let Joseph go. I made a mistake. But I enjoy Sam's company and we have so much in common. I guess I just need to move on.' Each time she went through it in her mind she reached a different conclusion.

Two days later Missy sat across from Sam on the Forthy Monkey porch watching the in crowd make their way to the shops and restaurants in the 12 South Area of Nashville as they waited for their salads. As Missy sipped her latte Sam laughed, "Look at that girl. Oh my."

Missy looked toward the street and asked, "What are you talking about. I don't see anything."

"You don't see that fat girl? How does she have the nerve to go out in public looking like that? Especially in this area. There is no way she could ever get enough to eat in these restaurants," Sam said as he laughed.

Missy sat shaking as his words echoed in her mind. It brought back so many memories of being treated like a freak in a side show in high school. Finally, she stood up and looked at Sam, "I made the wrong choice. I hope you have a good life but I am not going to be in it," as she spoke Missy walked away.

As she walked down the street she pulled her phone out and began calling Joseph but she got a message his phone was not working. Immediately she called Zeke, "I am trying to call Joseph but his phone is not working. Do you know how to get him?"

"I am having the same problem. I have been trying to get hold of him to tell him we are making a big profit in the security business but I get the same message. I have no idea where he is or how to reach him. I even asked Rose but she said he hung up on her and wouldn't loan her any money. That was all she knew."

Missy hung up the phone and went to her computer and began searching for Joseph Samuels but she couldn't find anything. Each night for the next three weeks Missy fell asleep with tears in her eyes. She had made a mistake and she couldn't undo it. She couldn't find Joseph.

Time passed slowly for Missy but it did indeed pass. Ten years later she was an emergency room doctor. She enjoyed the constant pressure of the emergency room so she accepted a position with the Vanderbilt Hospital in Nashville. Working nights Missy was dealing with gunshot wounds, heart attacks, and broken arms. She loved the constant change and feeling you got in the midst of the hectic pace of doing good for others.

Leaving work Missy made her way to her farm house outside of Franklin. She bought thirty acres with a barn and beautiful black board fence. Once she got home she went to the barn and got Beauty Two saddled and took her morning ride. A gate between the large horse farm to the west allowed Missy to go on long beautiful rides through green meadows. The neighbors encouraged Missy to put a fence in so she could ride their land.

Beauty Two was a Dark Chestnut Quarter Horse Missy bought after Beauty died. She had brought Beauty to Nashville and rented her a stable at a horse farm outside of Nashville. Age got the best of Beauty and finally Missy had to say goodbye to her oldest friend.

Missy dated some finding an interesting man from time to time but after a few dates she knew he wasn't the one for her and moved on to the next one. Growing close to thirty Missy knew she was reaching the time when she would either find someone to be her soul mate or spend the rest of her life alone. She often thought, 'Judging from the available men I am probably going to spend the rest of my life alone. After all what do I need with a man when I have my horse and my work.'

Arnold, her Father, was still working the farm trying to outdo the rest of the farmers in Southern Indiana and every year he continued giving the Harvest prayers. Jenny, his wife, gave up her singing career to be the biggest socialite in the county. She gave afternoon teas for those who she felt were worthy of her attention in the fall. At Christmas time she hosted a grand Christmas party with a swing band out of Louisville with a dinner catered by a restaurant from Indianapolis. Everyone wanted an invitation but only the 'right' people,' her words, were invited. The church folks were bothered by the rumors she served alcohol at the event, but the preacher said it was perfectly alright. Of course he got an invitation every year and he knew his job depended on saying whatever Arnold did was perfectly alright.

As time went by Jenny became so involved in her social world she was always tired when Arnold came around for sex. He started just looking at her to show he wanted it but when time passed he started begging her for it. Normally her response was, "Darling you know how much I want to but I am just worn out from everything I had to do today."

Arnold would go to his office and sulk the rest of the evening and when bed time came he would shower in the hopes she would relent, but before he could hit the covers she was sound asleep. Jenny had denied Arnold for seven months until one night after they returned from the rodeo at the county fair. There was something about seeing those cowboys that had got Jenny started so she grabbed Arnold and headed to the bedroom. After ten minutes of passion she noticed Arnold's breathing was short and as he turned from her he tried to get his breath but couldn't. Realizing the romp had been too much for Arnold she ran to call for help but by the time she got back to him, he was gone. Jenny told her friend, Sarah, "He just laid there with that goofy smile on his face."

Missy came back for the funeral. The line to the casket was outside the funeral home. Missy and Jenny both stood there as the people passed by saying how great a man he was. Jenny cried but Missy didn't as the people passed her. Jenny often talked about how great a husband he was and how much she would miss him. At the end of the line was a farmer from three farms down from Arnold's. As he approached, Missy finally blurted out, "He was what he was, a man who wanted something out of life I couldn't give him. He made my life miserable. But that was then and this is now, so we bury him and what we thought of him."

The farmer looked at Missy and said, "Darling we all are imperfect. We all hurt others and we all fail. The key is letting it all be buried tomorrow, don't carry it with you."

Missy watched as they lowered the casket and as others began to walk away she walked over and looked into the grave and said, "Good bye. It is over."

Missy continued working in the emergency room gaining a reputation as the best in her field in this part of the country. She got numerous offers from around the country with promises of more pay and less hours but she refused them. No one understood why but she did, deep down she hoped one day Joseph would return. But as time went by he didn't and she kept thinking maybe she needed to finally move on, find another place start a new life.

CHAPTER FOUR

Joseph graduated at the top of his class with a major in Philosophy and two minors, one in political science and the other in economics. With a degree in philosophy he knew he needed to get a masters and then a doctorate so he applied to Norte Dame and got admitted. Two years later he had his masters in philosophy and was prepared to seek a doctorate but he wanted somewhere new and different. Applying to several schools he finally got his first acceptance in the mail from Vanderbilt University in Nashville. He didn't respond waiting to hear from others, finally the one he was most interested in came, he was accepted to the doctorate program at Oxford in the United Kingdom.

Looking at the acceptance letter he rushed to respond, yes he would be there by next fall. He turned down Vanderbilt and headed across the pond to London. Spending several weeks in London as a tourist before he began his program at Oxford he was elated. There was Churchill's War Room, Royal Albert Hall, Tower of London, and Buckingham Palace. Joseph simply could not get enough of the city. Finally one evening he went to see, "The Play That Went Wrong," a English farce with broad humor. Sitting down he noticed the woman next to him with beautiful red hair and green eyes, he said, "Good evening."

She looked at him with his wavy brown hair now with small specs of gray around the temples, "Are you American?"

"Yes, I am. I suspect you are not."

"No, I am from here, a good citizen of London."

"Your date not here yet?"

"No, no my young American there is no date, I am on my own this evening. I have grown tired of the nonsense one has to put up with on dates. I have to eat some silly food that I don't like and laugh at his silly jokes. I prefer these days to spend them alone, especially seeing this play. I know this makes me ordinary but I love this play, it is so ridiculous."

"You have seen it before?"

"Oh yes three times. Now let me ask where your date is? And if you have none then I will be free to flirt with you in a good English woman way."

"I have no date so you are free to flirt."

"I trust you like the ladies?"

"I do, you?"

"No, I find them awful creatures. But I must say I can't say much for your gender either. I tell you what after the play you can buy me a drink at the pub on the corner and I will see if you are like the rest of the male species."

"I will buy you that drink and hope I meet with your approval."

After the play they made their way to the pub on the corner, sitting down in a booth in the back, she ordered a martini and he a Scotch on the rocks. She laughed as he ordered, "Oh I have a real American on my hands.

"I guess I am. My name is Joseph Buckley, what is yours?"

"Well Joseph my name is Darcy Huxley. My dear Mother read Jane Austen a good deal and thought I should carry that name around."

"Well it is a fine name, any relationship to Aldous?"

"No my American friend I am afraid not. Now we English girls think American men are either gay or cowboys. Which are you?"

"I'm not gay. I do live in Montana on a small plot of land with a beautiful horse, so I guess I am a cowboy. Not a good cowboy but a cowboy."

"What brings you to London?"

"I am starting a doctorate program at Oxford this fall, so I came early to play the part of the tourist. So what do you do when not attending plays?"

"Oh my an educated cowboy, the worse kind. Me, well I am afraid I am just a lowly teacher."

"Where do you teach?"

"Oh, at a drab old school."

"You know I will persist. So where is this drab old school?"

"Ok, I give, I teach history to a bunch of spoiled know it alls at Cambridge. Are you happy you made me confess my sins? Now tell me what do you intend to do with a doctorate from Oxford? Are you going to work for the CIA?"

"Good question. I suspect I will write a bit but beyond that I fail to see a reason for it. I hope my honesty does not offend you?"

"The one thing that will never offend me is honesty. I can deal with it, but deception I am afraid I cannot. I think Orwell learned that in his time. I hope you are not one of those communists, that would break my heart."

"I am many things but I am not a communist or socialist. I fight the battles I fight with reason and logic."

She paused a moment and finally she asked, "Have you been doing the tourist things?"

"Yes all the tourist points of interest."

"I think it is time for you to do some Londoner things. How about tomorrow I will show what we English do."

"That sounds great, what do you have in mind?"

"Sorry I cannot divulge that information at this time. Can you navigate the tube?"

"Yes, I have become good at getting around."

"Great take the Central line to Lancaster. You are staying down by the Buckingham, right?"

"Yes, great do that and I will meet you at the Lancaster Gate at 10:00am, Ok?"

"Yes, I will be there."

"Oh by the way, you will need to wear jeans and cowboy up."

"What are we doing?"

"Sorry I can't tell you. Meet me in the morning. Now I must go. I have enjoyed our talk."

"I have as well. I'll see you tomorrow morning."

The next morning Joseph thought about what she had said and decided he would do the cowboy up thing, so he put on his boots and black Stetson hat with his Wrangler Jeans and his western shirt with snaps. Standing at the Lancaster Gate the people hurrying to wherever they were going slowed as they passed. Some smiled a few giggled and a couple had something to say. Joseph just looked forward and ignored the comments and looks, they didn't matter to him. Finally Darcy walked up with a big smile in her skin tight pants, English riding boots, and a cap that said riding club. Her hair fell out of her hat down her back, Joseph was taken aback by how beautiful she was. His mind did not fully remember the beauty of her skin and the twinkle in her eyes, the flow of her red hair as it fell against her alabaster skin. And her body was perfectly shaped which she carried with an air of I don't care what anyone thinks, it made him smile.

"I think we are going riding."

"You Americans are so sharp," she laughed as they walked to Hyde Park.

The horses were selected for them. Darcy's horse was a gentle horse with no desire to do anything other than ride the trail. As Joseph got on his horse he realized the stable hand had decided to try and embarrass the American. His horse pulled to the right and then to the left as he refused to move forward. Quickly Joseph pulled the reins down showing his horse he was in charge. As his horse attempted to resist he pulled the reins around and forced him to proceed as ordered. Patting his horse on the neck, he reassured him they were in this together. The stable hand grumbled as Darcy and Joseph rode off.

As they finished their ride Joseph looked at Darcy and said, "Let's go another round."

"Sure, let's have a go at it," she said as they passed the stable hand.

Finishing their ride Darcy went to the stable's shop and brought back a basket. Holding it up she announced, "I have here our lunch, they provide as a part of the ride. Let' go over to the park and have a bit to eat."

Spreading the blanket Darcy said, "You know that stable hand was a bit cheeky. He thought giving you that horse would show you up, but you showed you are a real cowboy," she laughed as she got a bottle of wine out of the basket.

"Yes I know. But that is life. We all try to one up someone sometime along the way."

"My very mature of you," she said as she got the sandwiches out of the basket.

As they sat there on the Hyde Park grass looking at the horses and passersby Darcy asked, "Well my American friend I am afraid I do not know much about you. I think if I am to see ever to see you again I will need to know a bit of your story. What do you say? Are you willing to let me know who the real you is? Or perhaps you have no interest in seeing me again and see no need to bore yourself with details?"

"My, you are direct. First, let me say I do wish to extend our relationship. Is it alright that I call it a relationship?"

"You may unless you place obligations upon it."

"Very well our relationship without obligations. So I will gladly tell you my life's story. You will need to relax because it will take a bit of time," he said as he began to tell his story from his parents to the jail to Missy to Montana. He left nothing out going on and on.

Finally as he stopped he looked at Darcy, "Well now do you wish you hadn't wanted to know?"

"Now I know I am talking to an honest man. No liar would ever tell that story," she laughed.

"Yes, you are right no one with a bit of sense would have told what I told. I guess, if you must know I wanted you to know me, the real me. Now I need to know the real Darcy. The real person behind that beautiful red hair and face."

"Oh so we are trying flattery now to persuade the fair damsel? Well let me tell you about me. I was the only child to Samuel and Melinda Huxley in Salisbury. A small town where my Father ran his market and my Mother grew flowers to sell in his store. I worked there as a child and I must say I loved it. My Father and Mother loved knowledge and made it a point to provide me with books to read. Every night we would sit and read and then spend twenty minutes before going to bed telling what we had read that evening," Darcy stopped as she wiped a tear before going on, "I am sorry but it is such a wonderful memory. My childhood was ideal unlike yours. My Mother and Father died of age five years ago three months apart. My Mother died of cancer my Father of a broken heart. I do miss them."

"What a wonderful story. You had two great parents."

"Yes indeed I did. Now tell me as a student of philosophy what is your philosophy?"

"I haven't chosen one. I guess the best I can provide is a proscription at this moment. It should be the goal of all mankind to live as free as they can within the prison of their existence. That is it for the moment, perhaps I will fall on a philosophy somewhere along the way."

"Why haven't you found a philosophy you like?"

"Well this will seem odd but I find philosophies a sham."

"Wow, why do you think such a thing?'

"Look each philosophy is constructed backwards. They are formed to fit within the philosophers own life experiences. It is never new thinking it is an effort to develop a manner of thinking that fits themselves. As the philosopher once said, 'No man can think outside of himself,' so all thought is an illusion by a magician who tries to deceive the thinker."

"But some began believing something totally different than they professed earlier in their philosophical works."

"Nonsense, the seeds of doubt of their thoughts were sown years ago; again I say philosophical thought is a grand illusion."

"Wow telling your life's story and now your thoughts on your philosophical pursuits, I realize you are a brutally honest fellow. I must say I like it even though it does paint you as a very pessimistic person."

"I trust I am, but like the fools who think the way I think I say, I am realistic. But again honesty prevails here, that statement is a lie. There is no realism just an illusion created by our past projected on the present."

"Again an honest cowboy," Darcy laughed as she touched his arm.

"This day has been the best. I was wondering if you would like to see Andrea Bocelli in concert at The Royal Albert Friday?"

"Yes I would love to see him. How did you get tickets?"

"Well this old cowboy has his ways. The show is at eight, I can pick you up at seven."

"No, don't do that I will meet you at seven thirty in front of the Albert Gold Statue. Oh by the way you do know folks dress up for the Royal Albert?"

"Yes this old American cowboy knows."

Walking Joseph back to the tube station she touched his arm as she walked away with a smile. Joseph knew between now and Friday he had to get something proper to wear. He made his way to Harrods the next day buying a six thousand dollar Stefano Ricci suit, a one thousand dollar Dolce Gabba Sellter tie, and two thousand dollar Bottega Veneta leather shoes. Looking at in the mirror he thought, 'What a fool I am trying to impress a woman. Oh well, I am going to try to impress her anyway even if it is foolish.'

Darcy tried over the next two days different dresses with different shoes and different necklaces. No matter what the combination was she was displeased, but she continued to struggle to find something she liked. In the end she decided on a dress and necklace which hung down around her neck, she wasn't happy with it but she went with it as the best of them all.

The evening of the concert Darcy saw joseph standing by the Royal Albert Gold Statue. As she approached she saw his wavy brown hair neatly combed across his forehead and the gray around his temples in his black suit. She thought to herself, 'A little more gray hair and he would look exactly like Cary Grant.'

As Darcy approached Joseph struggled to get his bearings. She was wearing a silk black dress that flowed from the waist. Her eye brows highlighted the sparkle in her eyes. Her face glowed with innocence and certainty. He red hair flowed down her shoulders highlighting like a beautiful frame the extraordinary painting which was her face. As she approached he noticed the simple strand of pearls hanging down her front and realized what they were saying about her. The simple pearls pointed the way to her beautiful face; they were not to distract. Joseph needed to get control of his emotions as he walked toward her. He kept thinking her dress flowed and made her look like she was floating across the way to him, like a beautiful butterfly.

Approaching her he said, "Beautiful are you ready to head to our seats."

"Yes, handsome I am ready."

Taking her arm joseph pointed toward the side doors, "We need to go this way."

Darcy pulled back, "That is the way to the box seats. We need to go to the front."

"You underestimate this cowboy. We have box seats two boxes from the Royal Family."

"What, how did you manage that?"

"Never under estimate the cowboy," Joseph laughed as they made their way to the side doors.

Sitting down in their seats Joseph looked at Darcy, "You want to say hello to Prince William and Catherine?"

"Look cowboy we don't bother the Royal Family at these things. We aren't like Americans."

"Oh my you little English woman of little faith in this cowboy. I will be back in a moment."

A few minutes later prince William and Catherine walked in the room with Joseph. Darcy stood up and bowed and shuddered as she looked at the couple laughing with Joseph. Prince William stepped forward and said, "The Queen couldn't make it tonight so we have a couple extra seats why don't you join us."

Darcy was speechless trying to form words but she couldn't finally Joseph broke in and said, "We would love to join you. Come on darling." Sitting in the Royal box she whispered to Joseph, "You have a good deal of explaining after this is over."

Joseph smiled, "I will explain it my dear."

After the concert they walked a short way until they reached a small pub on a corner. The pub had a beautiful mahogany bar with friends and lovers sitting around the room in tall deep red leather wing back chairs around small walnut tables with brass legs. Sitting down in the chairs Joseph started to speak but the waitress was there at his side, so he ordered a martini for her and a scotch on the rocks for him.

As he sat back in his chair she said, "Ok enough, how in the hell did you arrange that tonight?"

Joseph laughed as he moved forward in his chair, "While I was a graduate student at Norte Dame I wrote a few articles that made their way to the magazine National Review. Three of those articles got reprinted here in good old England. Prince William read them and was impressed with the reasoning and logic as well as the brutal honesty. So, one day he called me to say just that and ask me to see him if I ever made it to London. I told him in fact I was coming the summer before starting my doctorate program at Oxford. He said great and we arranged to meet. We had a nice discussion disagreeing on most things but agreeing with the logic of the other. And then he offered me the tickets. So, there is the story."

"Well cowboy you do impress the ladies."

"That is my goal."

Sitting there for three hours they talked and talked and laughed as they grew closer. Finally, she said, "I must be getting home."

"Look I will get us a cab and take you to your place. Please let me be the gentleman."

"Very well, do the cowboy thing and take the little lady to her home."

As the cab pulled up to Culross street Joseph looked out the window and saw a beautiful white brick lateral house with three balconies and huge double doors. Turning to Darcy, "You must do real good teaching."

"Ok, I have a something I have not told you to this point. My Grandfather was a rather well known Barrister and made a good living.

When he died I inherited his estate. He didn't have a wife, some in the family felt he didn't care for women. Since I inherited it I just can't bring myself to sell it. His estate provides enough money to keep it going. Oh well I love it."

Joseph walked her to the front door and she stopped she looked at him and said, "I would love to ask you in tonight but I don't want it to be because it was a magical night and it was just that. I want it to be because I am in love with you. I hope you understand."

Looking into her eyes he leaned forward and kissed her and as he pulled back, "Yes, I understand. Thanks for going with me."

Slowly the rest of the summer they began to spend every moment together. Finally, one night Darcy looked at him and said, "Will you come in and have a drink."

Walking in Joseph thought this is a long way from the trailer he grew up in. Four levels a beautiful spiral staircase and a lift if you didn't care to walk up to bed. In the grand room just off the staircase was a beautiful Steinway Piano situated across from a mahogany bar and a large fireplace. The Steinway was a 1925 satin ebony grand piano. Joseph turned to Darcy, "Do you play?"

She looked back at him and said let me see as she sat down in front of the keys, "Now which ones of these sound the best, Hmm I wonder." Sitting there a moment she finally began to play Haydn Piano Sonata in D major and then suddenly she stopped and shifted to singing the "Look of Love" as she continued playing.

Finishing she turned to Joseph, "Let's go upstairs darling."

Walking into the bedroom he held her and kissed her deeply as they shared their passion. Stumbling to the bed she stopped, "I have fallen in love with you."

Joseph stopped a moment and smiled, "It is about time; I fell in love with you riding the horses."

The next morning Joseph rolled over to kiss her as she pushed away, "This isn't the movies. My breath is awful. Let me go brush my teeth."

"I guess I better also."

After brushing their teeth they held each other close and kissed, he looked at her, "You know we should be getting on with the day."

"To hell with the day. This is where I wish to be in your arms. Come climb on top and ride cowboy," she laughed as she kissed his neck.

Later they sat in robes with a pot of tea on the table and crumb cake. Turning to Darcy his smile turned to concern as he said, "You know in a short while we will be going off to Cambridge and Oxford. What are we going to do?"

"I have a place in Cambridge so you could come down each weekend and we could spend time together."

"I guess that will work. But I won't like be away from you all week."

"Nor will I my darling, but as soon as you get through the dreadful doctorate program we can be together all the time."

CHAPTER FIVE

The first two years were finished and the love between Darcy and Joseph grew stronger than ever. During Summer in London they made their way to Portobello to sample the food and look at the shops and vendors along the street with their antiques and works of art. As they passed a vendor with a tiny table with antique rings and bracelets spread out over a red table cloth, Darcy stopped and pointed to a simple diamond with a gold setting. The woman behind the table said, "Dear please pick it up and look at it. See if it fits. That ring came from a woman who lost her husband in the war. She wore it to the day she died. She asked that it not be buried with her but that it be sold to someone who appreciated it and was as much in love as she. She was my aunt."

Putting the ring on her finger she smiled with a glow as she touched it. Finally, she said, "What a wonderful story. This is the kind of ring I would love. I don't want some huge diamond that says I needed money to impress me, I want a diamond that is simple and says love to me. This ring says that."

Taking the ring off she handed it to the woman with a dejected look. Joseph stepped forward and said, "I want to buy the ring."

The woman smiled, "Wonderful."

Joseph handed her the money and as she started to put it in a box he said, "No need." Taking the ring he got down on a knee and said "Darcy you are the love of my life. Will you marry me."

Tears streamed down Darcy's face as she, "Yes, my love, yes I will."

They stood in front of the little table hugging as people passing by began to cheer. Finally Joseph looked at Darcy, "You have made me so happy. I love you."

The rest of the summer they spent going to plays and picnics and holding each other. They also spent their time reading during the evening before going to bed as they listened to Bach Harpsichord Music. Darcy at first wasn't a fan but as time passed she developed a taste for it. Some nights Joseph would share his political philosophy. Darcy listened but she wasn't really interested, she just knew he was.

The end of summer was always a sad time when they parted their ways with only the weekends to live for and Christmas break. Finishing his teaching assignment at Oxford for the semester he raced to his car that was already packed to make his way to Cambridge. They would have two wonderful weeks over the Christmas break, he so looked forward being with her.

Getting to her flat he walked in and saw her in a chair with ablanket covering her. Her face was white as she coughed. "Darling do you have a cold?"

"No, I don't know what is wrong with me. I just keep coughing and my chest hurts."

"Have you seen a doctor?"

"No, I haven't had time with my classes and the finals."

"Well we are taking you to a doctor tomorrow."

"That isn't necessary. Let's wait to see if it gets better."

"We are not waiting. We are going to tomorrow."

Appointments were made and finally late in the afternoon they were in the doctors examining room. The doctor recommended Xrays and a MRI. They were back in the office two days later waiting on him to make his way into the room to give the results. Finally, he walked in with her file and sat down by her and looked at the file. "There appears to be some spots on your lungs which may be cancer."

"That is silly. I have never smoked."

"Your file says your mother died from lung cancer. Sometimes it doesn't happen because you smoke. We need to do some more tests and make some decisions on treatment."

The tests and the endless doctor visits continued for the next three weeks. Finally, the news was grim. The cancer had spread through her lungs and there was nothing they could do.

"Nothing? You can do nothing except let her die, "Joseph yelled at the doctor as he heard the news.

"I wish I had better news but I don't. The cancer is too far advanced. She only has a few weeks to live. Chemo won't help it will just make her final days unbearable. We can admit her in a week or so or she can stay in her home if we can get her some help to assist with the final days.”

“Tell her not me. She is sitting right there it is her life you are dealing with, tell her damnit.”

“I realize this is difficult news but you must understand there is nothing else we can do.”

They drove home in silence and walked into the house. Finally Darcy said, “Come here and sit down a moment. We have some details we must discuss.”

“No we can’t discuss anything. If we do we are accepting it. No this isn’t final there is nothing to discuss. I will take you to a cancer clinic in America they will save you.”

“Darling don’t be foolish. I am not spending my final days away from my homeland. I am an English girl and I will die an English girl. Now if you love me you will sit down and go over the things I need to discuss.”

Joseph said nothing as he slumped into the chair looking at her through the moisture in his eyes. Finally, Darcy said, “First I am going to change my will so everything goes to you, the house and the money.”

“No don’t do that. I will never be able to stay here after you are gone. I can’t spend a moment in this house without you.”

“I understand. Sell it to someone who will take good care of it. There is no one else in the family to give it to, so please sell it. Now, I have to admit I am embarrassed to tell you I am a religious girl. I was raised in the Catholic Church so now facing the end I want to see my Priest. I hope you are not disappointed in me."

"Disappointed? There is nothing you could do which would disappoint me. I will gladly take you to your church tomorrow."

"Finally I will make arrangements for a final care nurse. She will make arrangements for the drugs and last moments."

Joseph couldn't take it anymore falling out of his chair grabbing her legs he sobbed uncontrollable, "Please don't leave me. Please don't. I can't live without you. I just can't go on. Please don't leave."

"Joseph you are a philosopher, you know life is what it is and death is a part of it. This would have been one day. You must go on and make me proud. Remember I am an English girl so be an English man cowboy for a while and have a stiff upper lip."

Joseph couldn't answer through the tears, he could only hold on as if he could keep her with him against all odds if held tight enough. Time though proved he wasn't able to hold her to this earth as she slowly slipped away. It was a quarter past nine on a Monday when she looked at Joseph and said, "It won't be long now. Go on to bed and I will go on as well in a bit."

"No my darling you are not leaving me without me being by your side."

Later the clock on the table chimed midnight and she was gone. Joseph, fell across her sobbing, "Darling, darling I love you. I love you."

A few days later Joseph was standing by the burial plot as the priest said a few words he didn't hear through the pain in his heart.

Finally they lowered her casket and Joseph was certain he would not be able to exist another moment as he fought throwing himself into the grave.

CHAPTER SIX

The annual Christmas party hosted by Doctor Wellington at his grand home on Westview Avenue in the exclusive Belle Meade area of Nashville was the event of the year for the hospital. Doctor Wellington had been quite successful in his career but it was his wife's money from family oil fields that bought the house and maintained it.

Missy loathed the event since it was an endless night of meaningless chatter by people who were slowly getting drunk. A jazz band with a beautiful young girl sang through the night fighting to be heard above the noise of the guests. Missy wished they would quiet so she could hear the music but it was a useless wish, the meaningless chatter was more important to them then beautiful music.

Doctor Lehman from pathology stopped missy as she crossed the room, "My dear beautiful Missy. I must ask while you won't let me get close to you. You are always so stand offish. I just want to be your special friend."

Missy looked at the drunk doctor and exhaled, "Perhaps it is because you are married."

"Oh my dear don't be so Victorian. We could have true bliss if you would just let go. I could make you very happy."

As she started to walk away he reached out and grabbed her arm pulling her back to him, "Don't walk away darling."

Suddenly, she felt an arm on her other shoulder, "Dear I have been looking all over for you. Come we must get a drink, Doctor Wellington wants to see us at once. Sorry old fellow but the lady is with me."

Walking away arm in arm she turned to him and said, "Who are you?'

He smiled, "I am Vic Strong. I heard that drunk fool was being a bore and thought I would rescue you. I hope you don't mind? How about that drink?"

"Thanks for saving me. The drink sounds great if we can go outside and get away from these people for a few moments."

"Sounds great."

Walking out to the patio area overlooking the pool they sat down with their drinks in hand. Finally she was able to see the man who had saved her, his hair was pulled back in a ponytail with a small scar on his cheek that seem to point to his dimples. His chin was narrow and with thin lips and brown eyes that sparkled. After evaluating him a moment she decided he was a very nice looking man.

"Now I do not remember ever seeing you in the hospital. What do you do?"

"I don't work at the hospital. I am a songwriter. The doctor invited me to add to the conversations among his guests."

"Have you written anything that made it to the radio?"

"Yes, I have had three songs that were number one on the charts. But I am not proud of those songs they were sell outs to make a living. The songs I am proud of no label will let an artist cut."

"Why?"

"Too dark; too damn truthful for pop country."

"Why are your favorite songs dark?"

"Because they are the honest ones. The rest of the crap is dishonest feel good nonsense."

"Why do you keep doing this if it makes you unhappy?"

"Good question. I have no idea."

Getting up Missy said, "Well thanks for saving me, I think it is time for me to head for home."

Vic looked up, "Would you like to go somewhere and listen to real music?"

"Not tonight but you can call me if you still want to in a few days."

"Great give me your number."

Two days later Vic picked her up and took her to a tiny bar with acoustic music performed by local songwriters. As they walked in Vic turned to Missy, "This is the one place we can come and play what really is in our souls, not that stupid fluff stuff. You won't hear songs about truck beds, beer, and red necks tonight, these will be real songs that have real meaning. Songs you will never hear on the radio."

"I still don't get it. Why do you continue to do this if it makes you angry all the time? Are you just wanting to be unhappy? Or is this some artistic thing that makes you feel better than others?"

Stopping Vic turned to Missy with a frown on his face, "Why you are direct and to the heart of the matter."

"I just want to know why someone does something that makes them angry or unhappy all the time."

As they sat down the waiter asked them what they would have. "Vic said a PBR please. How about you Missy?"

"White wine please."

As the waiter walked away Vic turned to Missy, "I don't have an answer. I understand your point. I guess I want to be an artist and real artists have to be unhappy warriors fighting against the system that belittles their art. I guess that is it."

Listening to the music Missy heard some beautiful lyrics squeezed between some boring attempts to say something the artist felt was necessary but couldn't find the words to say it. There was the constant chatter from the stage about the state of the music and their fight for the art. Missy felt a great sense of boredom with the constant theme of us against them, turning to Vic, "Well I think I should be getting home. You don't have to take me I will get a ride."

"Are you sure?"

"Yes, I have a busy day and I don't want that to ruin you night. Thanks for the evening."

Over the next two weeks Vic asked her out for another evening, but Missy had decided the artist was not the person she needed in her life, so she said no.

There were others that came and went over the years but there was always something about them that just didn't measure up. Some she broke their hearts while others hurt her. Carl Monday came into her life one evening in the emergency room when he was brought in with a cut on his arm. He had been rehearsing he stage show before they went out on tour and got too close to the edge of the stage most likely with too much gin in his system. Falling off the stage he cut his arm on a railing.

As Missy sewed him up he looked at her, "Darling you are good looking."

Sewing the last stitch Missy looked at him, "Thank you. You're not too bad looking yourself."

"Yeah that is what they all tell me. Want to go out and get a drink?"

"No, I have work to do."

"Well let me call you."

"I can't stop you from doing that."

Three days Carl called, "Darling this is Carl. How about you and I go to dinner tomorrow evening?"

"Where?"

"I will take you to the Palms. We can get in there without much fuss. How about it?"

"Ok pick me up at seven."

Carl Monday was at the top of country music with multiple number ones and sold out stadium concerts. He had come from a small town in Texas to Nashville trying to make it in the business, but all he heard was no from the corporate heads on Music Row. He paid his rent playing Honky Tonks around town until three in the morning and then went home washed got in bed and was up again at six that morning throwing his clothes on as he made his way to his job at Lowe's.

Weeks passed by followed by three years and the constant grind was finally taking its' toll. Most nights over the last year he had fallen into bed drunk waking with a headache and blood shot eyes. He realized chasing this dream was killing him. Finally one Saturday after playing his songs to two in the morning he walked up the street and sat behind a trash bin in the alley behind the Ryman, the former home of the Grand Ole Opry, pulling his gun out of his pocket. 'This dream is killing me. I best just speed the killing up,' he thought as he raised the gun to his head. Closing his eyes he pulled the trigger and a second latter looked in amazement at the gun thinking, 'How in the hell am I still alive. Why didn't the gun go off?'

Turning the gun over and over in his hand he finally realized he forgot to load it tonight. And then he remembered, 'I didn't have enough money to buy bullets. I am such a failure I can't even afford to the bullets to kill myself.'

Getting up he began to walk down the alley toward the street putting his gun back in his pocket when a man approached. "You are Carl aren't you?"

"Yes, I know you think I am going far. Well I am not. Bye."

"Look I am Warren Finn from Mega Label. I have been watching you these last two weeks and I think you have real potential. I want you to come to my office Monday at ten and we will talk."

"Sure sure, I'll be there Monday. Sounds great."

Monday lead to a recording contract, which lead to stardom for Carl. The only issue was Warren demanded complete control. The result was Carl became a packaged commodity from clothes, to hair, to music. He became what Warren envisioned he should be to make him marketable singing songs Warren said the young girls from eleven to sixteen wanted to hear. His fame lead him to stadium shows where he sang and danced across the stage gyrating in front of the screaming young girls.

Warren demanded total and complete control to the point of where he lived. Warren wanted to buy a condo in Nashville but Warren demanded he buy a place outside of town with sixty acres and horses. As Warren pointed out, "You have to look country even though the songs you sing don't sound much like country songs."

Carl often asked, "Why don't I just sing some songs that are country?"

"Because you need to sing songs you are known for and the girls want you to sing."

Carl was now entering his sixth year atop the Country Music totem pole. People magazine ran a six page story on him entitled 'King of Country Still.' The photos in the article showed Carl with his three horses and dog McIntosh. The quotes ran from I love country music to I am humbled by my fans. The article ended with the quote from Carl, "Every day I give thanks to God for all I have. I just want to give back to all who have supported me all these years."

Carl pulled up in front of Missy's Franklin home in his King Ranch with boots, blue jeans, blue blazer and a large gold belt buckle. Carl stood six foot four with black hair pushed back from his forehead with a narrow chin and eyes that sparkled. Reaching the door he knocked and waited until finally Missy opened the door wearing a red dress that slid down her body reaching her ankles with a gold necklace with one tiny cross.

Making their way to downtown Nashville to the Palms they stopped as a valet rushed up to the truck saying, "Mr. Monday, great to see you. I'll park your truck in a special place."

Carl laughed, "Son, my Father was the Mr. in my family, I am just Carl. Here take this," Carl said as he handed him a $100.

"Wow Carl thanks."

Sitting down at a table toward the back of the dining room they picked up the menus as the waiter rushed to them. "Carl your usual and how about the lady?"

"Yes my usual but make it a double. Missy how about you?"

"I am going with water for the moment."

As they began to look at the menus the manager walked up to them. "I am so happy to see you again."

"It is great to be here again."

The manager leaned forward, "Carl I trust we won't have a repeat of the last time."

"No repeat."

"Excellent it is great to have you here."

As the manager walked away Missy asked, "What was that all about?"

"Well funny thing the last time I was here I was with the fellows in the band after a rehearsal. We got a little wild and got into some trouble."

"What did you do?"

"Not sure but according to the bill I saw we caused six thousand dollars of damage."

"Well let's make sure that doesn't happen tonight."

"Will do."

Missy asked, "How do you like being a Country Music Star?"

"Well I like the money and the fact it is easy to get laid."

"What?"

"It is easy to get laid. The women slash girls are lined up wanting to bed me. I don't have to put any work into getting one into bed."

"Changing the subject, how do you like your horses?"

"Horses?"

"Yes, horses. I saw the People Article and the photos of your horses and that beautiful dog, McIntosh."

Carl leaned back in chair laughing as he took a long drink of his Scotch. "All of that is PR bull. You can't believe that nonsense."

"Really?"

"Yes, every time they do a photo shoot the label brings in horses and that stupid dog. I am afraid of horses and I sure don't like dogs. You will find I am nothing like what they say I am. I am just a walking talking figment of the label's imagination. They dress me, tell me what to say and how to say it, they tell me where to live, they taught me how to walk and how to speak with a bigger Texas accent. They paid my family to not take interviews about me because they don't fit the mold of a Texas country boy and they were afraid they might tell the truth. Finally they tell me what to sing and I hate those songs. So you see there is nothing real about me, I am just a lie."

"Why do what they say?"

"I like the money and I like getting laid. Look I am a weak man. I hate it that I am so damn weak, but I am. So, I jump when they say jump and on the way up I ask high how am I to land?"

"It just seems like an awful way to live life. You have enough money by now why not demand to do the songs you want to sing the way you want to sing them?"

Carl grabbed a pin and began to draw on the white table cloth, "You are going to ruin the table cloth. They won't like that."

"Nonsense, I will sign it and they will make money selling it to some stupid fan."

Carl pointed at his drawing, "This is a cliff and the artist is on the edge of that cliff their entire career. One false step and they fall off that cliff. It could be a bad album or bad interview, or waiting too long to introduce new music. It can be anything that causes you to fall off the cliff. Once you fall you never make it back to the cliff because there is someone standing where you were. After that you spend your efforts trying to keep the band paid by working casinos but you can't afford the same big band. Without the backup singers and extra instruments people begin to hear how poorly you actually sing these days and you begin to lose access to the good casinos. I like the money and getting laid. I don't want to fall off the cliff."

"Then quit complaining. You have chosen what you want so deal with it."

"I didn't figure you would understand."

Finishing their meal Carl ordered his third Scotch and smiled at Missy, "You are good looking. Doctors aren't normally good looking. What do you say we go back to my place and take a dip in the pool."

"I don't have a suit with me."

"We won't need suits darling. Then once we are refreshed from the swim I can show you my bedroom."

"No, I think not. I am not one of your adoring fans. I would need time to get to know you better."

"Well doc that is not a good answer. You know you want to bed me so just let go and let's get it done. After all I don't take many out for dinner, so you should show some appreciation."

"Carl, I am going to give you the benefit of the doubt and say the Scotch is talking right now. I am not going to your place now or ever."

"Very well. I will have Lee take you home. I am going to stay and talk to that waitress."

"I will find my own ride you drunk ass."

As Missy walked out of the Palms she heard Carl yell, "Hey get that pretty waitress over here."

CHAPTER SEVEN

Joseph made his way to the airport trying trying to push everything from his mind but still Darcy creeped in and he began to cry. It had been five years since she died but the pain was as if it were yesterday. The home was sold and estate settled now with his Doctorate in hand he was headed back to Montana. He had kept only one thing from the house, her piano. It was to be shipped as soon as he found a place for it.

He made his way to his old home outside of Helena where the renters were waiting. Knocking on the door they opened the door and he saw the entire family standing in a group, Mother, Father, Daughter and Son all looked at him with sadness in their eyes.

Walking into the room Walterd Smithwell said, "Please come in and have a seat."

His wife told the kids to go outside and enjoy the air, and then asked, "Would you like a water or something?"

"No, I am fine," Joseph said as he sat back in his old leather chair.

Walter seemed uneasy having not seen his landlord in seven years. When they moved in his daughter was seven and son was five. For seven years they had lived here and made a home but now they were going to have to move and return the place to Joseph.

Joseph asked, "How is my dear horse?"

"He is doing great. We added three horses so we could take rides together."

"Great, well I need to get right to it. Sorry but I just don't have a lot of time. I have decided to find a place in Bozeman so I won't need this place."

"I understand. I wish we could buy it but I doubt we could afford it."

"That is fine because I am not selling it. I am giving it to you. All I ask is you continue to take care of my horse."

"What? Give it to us? I can't believe it."

"Well believe it. I don't need the place or the money so I have deeded it to you. Here is the deed."

"I don't know how to thank you. Thank you."

His wife ran to the door yelling, "Kids come quick. We aren't moving."

Joseph left with a smile on his face knowing what it meant to the family but still deep inside there was a hole and nothing could fill it.

Going to Bozeman he found a contemporary home on 150 acres with large floor to ceiling windows so from every point in the house you could see the mountains beyond the green fields. He had the barn rebuilt to house four horses although he only bought two. He found an old refurbished red 65 Ford F-150 online and had it delivered. Then he had the piano delivered from England and placed it in front of the study window.

Several colleges called wanting him to come to their schools but he declined. He told them he was simply not in the right state of mind to teach. He spent his time writing for National Review and other publications. Basically he wrote for anyone who was willing to publish his work. Over the first year back from England he began to receive requests to come and speak. Finally, he accepted six and made his way to the Midwest to speak.

His first speaking engagement was Norte Dame before a Conservative group. The second was at Indiana State before another Conservative club. Finally, he spoke at Hillsdale College before a mixed crowd. The first two events drew protestors but none showed up at Hillsdale College a Conservative institution.   The protests were against him as a Conservative, which had nothing to do with anything he had ever said or written.

The final speaking engagements were cancelled due to the protests. Returning to Montana he wrote a long article that ended up in several publications entitled, "When did we Redefine Intellectualism?" In the article he argued we have returned to the definition of intellectual used in the Dark Ages. It is no longer open minds open to ideas that challenge but is closed minds willing to place the offending party at the stake in the city square to burn.

The article was discussed but it changed nothing and speaking engagements did not come flooding in from the fearful Universities. Finally, he received a request to speak at the Midwest Conservative Conference in Louisville, Kentucky.

Joseph arrived early to the conference so he could go across the river and make his way to his old home town area. He didn't miss it but he did wonder what it was like these days. Driving into Covington he saw the same buildings that were there when he left with little change except for possibility a new awning or sign. Stopping at the small convenience store where he had spent time at as a youth, just hanging out, for a water he saw a woman behind the counter with bright yellow hair and a tattoo down her neck. As he approached her he realized it was Rose. "Rose do you recognize me?"

"Why it is that no good Joseph. How you been?"

"I have been great. You?"

"I am working at the convenience store. It doesn't get much better," she laughed.

"How is the rest of the family?"

"Oh my they are still performing daily all around town. Devon had to give up the Moses act. He didn't pay his taxes on the money he collected so they sent him away for two years. The bad thing is one of his gimmicks was to be healed they should show faith by throwing their medicine on the stage. Well they found as they investigated him for tax fraud he was selling the drugs on the street, so he got six more years. He is out now but he doesn't work. He started a church out in the country and is living off those people. The rest are like me as crazy as ever. You did good getting away from this."

"I guess I did. Rose it is good to see you again. I am going down the road to see the old trailer."

"Oh, that ain't there any longer. They built an apartment complex for the elderly down there."

"Rose nice seeing you again. I guess I'll be leaving I have to get ready for a talk in Louisville. Take care."

"See you, by the way you did right not giving that money for drugs. They busted some of the guys selling on the square and I would have been there right with them again."

Joseph drove down Interstate 65 toward Louisville as the past walked through his mind. Things he hadn't thought of in years raced through. The first time he met missy and the last time he saw her gave him a slight shudder. The night his Father got blown to bits trying to steal Arnold's money. The time he spent in jail and the day he picked up William F. Buckley Jr's book, 'Did You Ever See a Dream Walking'. Maybe he could incorporate that memory into his speech, but doing so would require telling his entire history. The history before becoming a Buckley, maybe it wasn't wise.

It was Saturday night, time for the final speech of the conference before everyone headed for home and Joseph had been given the honor of addressing the three thousand. Senators, Congressmen, the Vice President, several Conservative Thinkers, and various television Conservatives had spoken during the conference and now Joseph had the honor of the final speech.

Joseph wrote his speeches in his mind for days and then put them on paper. But, he never read them, he gave them from memory which sometimes meant he went in directions he did not anticipate going. This night his speech was simply entitled 'Intellectualism the danger of a Leftist Definition.'

Joseph's speeches were short and concise. He often argued long speeches were a waste in the modern age. He pointed out, "No one is able to maintain interest in anything beyond fifteen minutes." So he prided himself in speeches that were precise and to the point.

Ending his speech he stood accepting the applause as he walked away from the podium. In the distance he heard the sound of an explosion and in that instant he felt a sharp pain in his arm. The force of the object hitting his arm pushed him backwards causing him to fall hitting his head on the stage. Laying there trying to understand what had happened he struggled to get up but he felt weak and fell back. Realizing the object that struck his left arm was a bullet he felt for the blood which now was flowing down his arm. He could hear in the distance what sounded like mass confusion but he had difficulty focusing on the sounds. He heard someone yelling, "He has been shot", while another voice in the distance yelled, "We have the shooter."

Maybe it was shock or just the moment whichever Joseph began to laugh, "I got shot telling people to open their minds to ideas. What an age." Someone applied a belt to his arm to slow the bleeding and another held his head saying, "The ambulance is on the way."

Soon the paramedic was lifting him into the back of the ambulance saying, "Please relax, you are going to be fine."

On the way to the hospital he heard voices as if they were coming from somewhere away giving orders. The voices said something about his blood pressure saying, "Give him a shot." As shot of what he did not know. It was as if he was a bystander unable to participate in the drama looking outside of himself at the confusion.

He kept thinking, 'I was just shot in the arm, I will be alright.' But the voices seem to be saying something different. The shouting told him it wasn't just a simple shot to the arm, he was in some kind of danger. But he couldn't focus fully on what was going on around him. The shouts from the paramedic by his side about blood pressure told him something was wrong something was not right, he needed to be concerned but he just didn't have the energy to do anything other than listen to the noise around him.

As he laid there he heard the ambulance siren and wondered how long would it be until they got there. As the ambulance turned a sharp corner blasting its' horn he felt weak and began to slowly drift away. As he drifted he saw a face in the distance. His heart leaped with joy, "It's Darcy."

Racing to her he threw his arms around her filled with joy. She held him close and finally she pulled away, "Joseph my darling, your time is not now. You have a life to live.'

"I don't want to leave you. I want to stay with you."

"Darling there is love for you still in the future. You must let go and go on with your life."

"I can't love another ever again."

"You can and you will. I love you darling but I want you to live your life. Live it and love again. Go back, I see love waiting for you."

"But if I love again I will being pushing you aside."

"Nonsense darling. You have room for love of more than one."

"I love you, please don't make me go."

"I love you and I will love you living your life with love once again. God Bless darling."

"Please let me stay."

Suddenly, Joseph's body shook from the effects of a shot into his heart as he heard a voice say, "I have a beat. I have a beat. Get this damn ambulance to the hospital."

CHAPTER EIGHT

Missy made her way home through the traffic tired looking forward to spending time at home. She had spent the last twelve hours dealing with issues in the emergency room between nurses and doctors and the XRay Department. Every part of the hospital the Emergency Room touched involved massive egos that had to be massaged. She longed for the day when she just practiced medicine. Now in her new position in charge of the Emergency Department she was a diplomat and psychiatrist and mediator and a boss.

Worse than being a psychoanalyst, she had to be a defender. Some doctors saw the nurses as a group of possible sexual conquests. The nurses felt that was unfair unless she wanted to be a conquest. As a result Missy was constantly dealing with the sexual advances of horny doctors. Most times it took getting both parties to mediate the problem so it didn't go on a permanent record .

Finally Missy was home with her horse and the quiet of her home. It was too late to take a ride so she fed Beauty 2 and brushed her thankful she had the rest of the evening off from the emergency room. Walking from the barn her phone began to ring, answering she said, "What is going on."

"There have been two shootings downtown. The victims are on the way here, the CEO thinks you need to be there. Apparently at least one of the people shot was important."

Missy shut the phone and made her way to her car. 'So much for relaxation.' As she arrived at the emergency room she asked the nurse on duty, "What famous person has been shot"

The nurse looked up from the chart with a look of anxiety, "Carl Monday was shot in the chest by a band member. Apparently his drummer found him in bed with his wife so he shot him. Carl got a couple shots off as well. He hit the drummer in the leg and groin."

"How are they doing?"

"Carl went into shock and they are trying to stabilize him. They took him up to surgery but until they get him calmed down they can't do anything. The drummer is just angry and appears he will be alright. By the way there are several reporters outside wanting details."

"I am going up to surgery. Tell the reporters to go to hell."

Walking into the operating room she saw they were still concerned with getting him stable so they could continue. Finally, the surgeon said, "We have no choice if we wait any longer he dies. We have to proceed. Does everyone agree." Everyone voiced their agreement and the surgeon turned to the anesthesiologist, "Doctor we need your best work. Anything less and he dies."

Missy walked out realizing there was nothing to do except deal with the public information issues. Three hours later surgery ended and the wait to see if they had saved or killed Carl began. Missy told the waiting press there was no story here and went on to say, "Carl Monday had underwent surgery and his outcome was unknown at this time."

A reporter asked, "Who shot him?"

"Well as you can see I am a doctor in charge of the Emergency Room, so that question needs to be addressed to the proper authorities. I will only be able to give you information about the time he was in the emergency room."

In the Baptist hospital Emergency Room in Louisville Joseph was in the care of Doctor Stevens, a kind gentleman. As Joseph was stabilized Doctor Stevens began to tell him, "Son you will be alright. You lost some blood but the injury was not life threatening. There was some crazy moments getting you here but now we have everything under control. You went into shock and your heart stopped for a moment. But you are doing great now."

Joseph looked at the doctor through a haze wishing he could go back to Darcy, "Thanks doctor. I appreciate what you have done."

They took Joseph to a room and as the nurse gave him a shot checking his pulse he cried thinking of the last moment he saw Darcy. 'Why do I have to live when she was there waiting.'

The next few days he was visited by various Conservatives as he continued to gain strength. His story had been on the 24 hour networks as they argued who was to blame. CNN and MSNBC blamed him for stirring hate while FOX blamed the Left for the hate. As Joseph laid gaining strength he asked himself, 'Why it is so hard to blame someone for what they did.'

Growing stronger he asked for his laptop and began to write a piece entitled, "We Disagree." In the article he argued we are different, some white, some black, some yellow, some Christian, some Jew, some Hindu, some atheist, and some don't know so why can't we celebrate our diversity. He asked the question, "Why can't all diversity be cherished?" He knew as he wrote the words he was talking to a world existing in a wind tunnel called Twitter, no one heard anyone there. They heard the faint sounds of the echo against the walls in a tunnel of noise.

Missy decided the day was ruined for her so there was no reason to go home, so she went to a room just off the emergency room ward and laid down on the cot. Fifteen minutes later a nurse was shaking her, "Doctor there are some reporters that wish to see you."

Rolling over she said, "Tell them to get back with me tomorrow when I might give a damn. No, wait tell them to quit bothering me." Realizing she was not going to get any sleep she made her way upstairs to see if Carl was alive or dead. Checking with ICU she learned Carl was alive in room 11. Walking down the hall she saw five in men suits outside his room. Going back to the nurse she asked, "Why in the hell do you have five men outside his room?"

"They said they needed to talk with him?"

"I don't care what they need. Get them out of there immediately."

Standing there she waited while the nurse ran down the hall to tell the gentlemen they had to leave. As she waited she heard voices demanding they be allowed to stay so she walked down the hall to the men in suits. "Look you all have to leave."

"Do you know who we are?" One of the men said as he raised his voice.

"Look I don't care who you are. You cannot be here and if you don't get your dumb asses out of here I am calling the swat team to come in here and remove you. So, you bloated over important men in suits go now."

As they began to walk away one said, "I will be telling the CEO of my treatment."

Missy laughed, "I can walk you up to his office if you like."

The man said nothing and continued to walk away. As they left Missy went in to check of Carl. As she entered the room Carl smiled, "I guess I stepped off that cliff."

"Yes, I think you did."

"Those suit people were trying to figure out a way to spin this in my favor. They wanted to put out a release saying I was praying with Leah. Do you believe that? They said Leah was demanding $550,000 to go along with the story. And, better yet Logan, the man who shot me, said he had to have $500,000 to go along with the story. These people are amazing."

"What are you going to do?"

"Nothing, I figure it would be nice to be honest once in my life."

"Good for you Carl, now you need rest."

Two weeks later Carl walked out of the hospital to a throng of reporters. His stadium shows had been cancelled and the label told him it was over. They said they would wait a month to make the announcement so he could resign from the label saying he was going to rehab or something like that. Carl told them, "Cancel me out now."

Six months later Carl sat by his pool looking at the bills that were piling up and walked out on the diving board and sat down. As he looked at the water beneath him he raised the gun to his temple and pulled the trigger. They found his bloated body floating in a pool of blood two weeks later.

Joseph walked out of the hospital to a rental car and decided he would drive to the ocean to Rosemary Beach. Maybe sitting and reading listening to the waves of the ocean would soothe him. He thought, 'I have to find a way to move on but how can I?' Deep down Joseph knew he was struggling to find a way to exist, a way to live with the pain he felt.

Driving down Interstate 65 be began to feel weak. He noticed he had broken out into a sweat as he wiped his forehead. Making his way around Nashville he was getting faint. Stopping the car along the interstate he struggled to get control of himself but now he was passing out for a few moments at a time. Finally, he saw a red light behind him and could see the officer approach, "Sir are you alright? Are you having car trouble?"

"No car trouble but I have become faint and I am passing out for a few moments at a time."

The officer leaned close to Joseph to smell his breath and then said, "I will call for help. Just be calm."

In a few moments he could hear the sound of an ambulance as it approached. Then a paramedic was at the window asking confusing questions. They were confusing because he was sliding in and out. The trip in the back of the ambulance was a blur as it sped weaving through the traffic. Reaching the emergency room they wheeled him to bed eleven down the hall and immediately the nurse began taking vitals and asking a series of questions. The nurse stationed at the front desk buzzed Missy who was in the lounge eating, "A Joseph Buckley has been brought in. He is the Conservative fellow that was shot a couple weeks ago. He is in bed eleven."

Missy put her sandwich down and made her way down the hall to the ER thinking, 'Another celebrity, just what I don't need.'. As she passed approached bed eleven she took the chart hanging on the wall and began to read. The nurse's diagnosis was infection from the wound to the arm. Grabbing the curtain that hid the bed missy walked in, "Mr. Buckley I am Doctor Richman," she said with her head bent looking at the chart and then she lifted her eyes. There in the bed was Joseph Samuels not Joseph Buckley. "Joseph?"

"Oh my Missy."

"This says your name is Buckley."

"I changed it long ago. I didn't like being a Samuels."

"That is why I couldn't find you."

"You tried to find me?"

"Yes after that day at the coffee shop I realized I had made a big mistake. Did Zeke ever get hold of you?"

"No, I forgot about Zeke. Why did he want to get hold of me?"

"The business was doing great and he wanted to send you some money."

"So you made a big mistake, interesting," Joseph smiled as he looked at Missy.

"Yes, but don't press it. I will have to quit being honest if you do."

"No problem."

"First things first we need to deal with your wound. It appears you have some infection so we will clean the wound and give you something to help fight the infection."

"Thanks, you know I have missed you."

"I am your doctor now so listen you have to take better care of the wound. I missed you as well. I am going to have you admitted for the night and if everything looks good we will release you in the morning. They will take you up and you can get some rest. I will see you in the morning, but first here is my number and you give me yours. Don't change your number!"

The next morning Joseph was putting his shirt on when Missy walked into the room. She looked at him with a smile holding his chart, "Well it appears everything is in order here. Now again that wound needs to be cared for properly."

"Yes doctor I will follow your instructions."

Missy paused a moment looking down at the floor and then at him, "I was thinking you should stay here a few days so we could spend some time catching up. After all Christmas is two weeks away and you don't want to spend it alone on the ocean, do you? Oh wait I am being foolish you may be spending time with someone there, how silly of me."

Joseph laughed, "No one waiting on me down there. You know I think that is a good idea. We need to do some talking."

"You can stay with me, if you want."

"Thanks but I will stay at a hotel so I won't be in your way."

 "I get off at five. You want to get together then."

"Sure, name the place and I will be there."

"How about the Hemingway Bar on Houston Street?"

"Hemingway, sounds great. Is seven ok?"

"Yes that is great. I'll meet you there."

Walking into the Hemingway bar Joseph sat down waiting for Missy, afraid she wouldn't come.

Looking up as he sipped his drink he saw Missy walking toward him in a black dress that clung to her body and flowed from her waste. She looked like a butterfly as she walked toward him as the skirt swirled around her. Looking at her he noticed the pearls that hung around her neck way that seem to say nothing should hide the beauty the was beyond. "I hope you haven't had to wait long."

"No, only had time for one drink waiting in anticipation of the beautiful Missy."

As they sat down she asked, "Why have you always thought I was beautiful?"

"Well, because you are. There was always something about you that was honest and real. Yes you were heavy once but you were still beautiful to me. I saw in those eyes a person that was honest and real and there is nothing more beautiful than that. And, I also saw that first day in those eyes someone who had been hurt and it broke my heart."

"I want you to know how much your friendship meant to me. How much it meant that you protected me and showed me such wonderful friendship. Because of you I survived that life and made it here to this point."

"I am happy I was there for you. But you need to understand I never saw you as just a friend. I realize that is how you see me, but I always saw you as someone I loved."

Missy sat for a moment as she wiped the moisture from her eyes, "You were far more than a friend, you were someone I loved and it broke my heart when I couldn't reach you. I was desperate and my heart was broken when I realized I had lost you. I tried so hard to find you."

"So where do we go from here?"

Missy thought a moment as she leaned forward across the table, "We go wherever this leads us. We follow our hearts to the end of this.

I don't know what the end for us is but I am certain I want to find out what it is."

"Sounds good to me, so let's order and start this relationship as if this is the beginning."

The evening went by so fast as they talked about their lives over the past several years. Joseph talked of Darcy and the pain and his efforts to find a way to move forward. Missy talked of her career and the inability to find anyone that measured up to what she wanted in a man.

Joseph told of his Montana ranch and horses and Missy talked of Beauty 2 and her other two horses. Missy told Joseph how every year she had worked through the holiday so others could have the time off but his year she decided she would take two weeks off and try to reconnect with Christmas. "There was a time when I was a little girl that Christmas was a magical time for me. But as I grew older and fatter and my Father grew further from me I began to hate it. I remember one Christmas our cook fixed Christmas cookies and I was excited gobbling them down in the kitchen when my Father walked in. He threw the cookies in the trash and yelled, "You're too damn fat to be eating cookies." That was the end of my loving Christmas. So I made my mind up this year I was going to find the Christmas joy again and like magic you showed up, a Christmas miracle," Missy sat back in her chair with a big smile on her face.

"Did you ever wonder why as soon as you left your home you lost weight?"

"No, I knew all along. I was miserable there and the worse I felt the more I ate. When I got to Belmont I was free of them and I was happy. The people I met here loved me for being me not for what I looked like and as soon as I began to feel their love the weight came off."

"Well you look great. But, of course to me you have always looked great. I forgot to ask whatever happened to your Mother and what about the farm."

"My Mother has a huge oil business in Southern Illinois with a large mansion on five hundred acres. She married Stu Wheeler an oil man from a small town over there, I think it was Irvington. Any way Stu and her are happy as can be. She sends me a card on my birthday but she never calls. Whatever happened to your family?"

"Well of course my Father ended up in pieces on your Father's farm and the rest of the Samuels are basically like they always were, half crazy. But I must admit I really don't know for sure, the only one I have talked with in the past several years is Rose."

"Does it bother you someone would shoot you?"

"Well it doesn't make me particularly happy. But, I am not changing who I am or cowering in a corner afraid to speak freely."

"I read where one of the groups said you were a racist. Is that true?"

"No, that is not true. That is the technique of the leftists. They call you a racist or homophobe and you are instantly put on the defense. Some try to appease them making grand gestures to the leftist but it never works. The other aspect of this method is it allows them to refuse to listen to your position on issues. They say, 'We should not be listening to racists' and thus they argue it gives them the right to stop you from speaking. They are Marxist and they use these techniques to stop anyone from expressing a view contrary to theirs. Now so we are clear you can read every article or speech I have written or spoke and you will never find one word that is racist."

"Does it frustrate you?"

"It angers me that a portion of the population is willing to deny free speech to others. When I left to study at Oxford intellectualism meant one had an open mind to different views and sought an understanding of them, now it is the exact opposite."

Missy looked at the clock on the wall and sighed, "I had no idea it was this late. It is quarter past two."

"Oh my, I had no idea either. We best be leaving."

"Look I was thinking there is a big Christmas party tomorrow night. A doctor puts it on every year, why don't you go with me, please."

"Alright. Is that part of your effort to get in the Christmas spirit?"

"Yes, I am even going to get a tree and put something on it. I guess I will have find something to decorate it with. I'll pick you at your hotel at seven."

"Wait how dressy is this thing. I don't have any real dress clothes."

"Don't worry about it. Just wear whatever."

CHAPTER NINE

Joseph looked through his suitcase and realized the nicest thing he had were some blue jeans a blue blazer white oxford shirt his Lucchese boots and a belt adorned with silver dollars. Looking at what he had he laughed, 'They are not going to like me but I am not buying clothes to impress them.'

Missy called up and waited for Joseph to make his way down the elevator. As he walked off the elevator toward her she smiled thinking, 'Wow he looks like a confident real man.'

As Joseph grew closer to Missy he simply exclaimed, "Wow you are beautiful." She stood there in a red skirt down hung to her knees showing her curves with a white blouse and a black cardigan cashmere sweater. Joseph stopped again and said, "I have to say it again. You look beautiful."

Missy smiled looking at Joseph with hair slightly gray around the temples pushed back across his forehead and his narrow chin and piercing eyes, "You look mighty nice."

Getting to the front of the mansion the valet ran out to the car taking the keys. As she handed him the keys she asked, "Still waiting on that music deal?"

"Yes, I may be close but close doesn't pay the bills."

"Well I want free tickets when you start your tour," Missy said handing him a twenty.

He laughed taking the money, "You get front row seats."

As they walked toward the door, "He is trying to make it in the music business. Good kid, I hope he gets it done. But, I guess that could be the worse thing for him. They often find fame isn't all they thought it would be. Oh well he is a good kid."

Walking in the front door a man stood asking for their invitation and pointing them toward the great room where the music was coming from. They made their way through the foyer to a large open room with marble floors and a thirty foot ceiling with a small band on a stage in front of the massive window that looked out into the dark of night. As they approached the room they saw a large mahogany bar across the side of the room with a man and woman handing out drinks. Making their way to the bar their journey was interrupted by a woman in a long blue gown and a diamond necklace. Her face looked like it was the last failed effort of a mad science trying to take the wrinkles of time away with a snip here and there. Botox had failed her and the mad scientist had as well leaving a disfigured character from Batman in her place. No one said what they saw, no one told the king he had no clothes, rather they lied telling her she looked beautiful. As she approached the woman without wrinkles said, "Darling Doctor Richman so glad you made it. Now who is this cowboy?"

"This is a good friend of mine, Joseph Buckley."

"The racist that got shot?" she said as she turned to look at him as if she could see his racism across his face.

Missy started to speak but Joseph interrupted her, "It is nice to be here. Such a lovely setting."

She looked as Joseph extended his hand as if she took it she would be pulled into some racist web. Finally not taking his hand she turned to Missy, "Please enjoy," as she walked away.

Joseph turned to Missy, "There you have the uninformed. Simply accepting a narrative created by the Leftist. Oh well so be it."

Walking across the room Dr. Logan a surgeon rushed over to Missy, "Doctor I am so happy to see you. They tell me you are actually taking a couple weeks off."

"Yes, I am going to enjoy Christmas this year."

"Good for you. Who is this young man?"

Missy didn't want the same result as the last introduction but she went ahead, "This is a very good friend, Joseph Buckley."

"Oh my you are the young man that got shot. I love your articles. They are so well argued and researched. It is great to meet you."

Joseph smiled, "Thank you. I appreciate that."

Dr. Logan grabbed Joseph's hand and said, "Dr. Richman do you mind if I steal your friend for a few moments? I want to introduce him to some people across the room."

"Very well but don't keep him away from me for long."

The doctor escorted to a group close to the bar and introduced him. Immediately they wanted his take on a wide range of subjects. Finally, Joseph stopped his comments saying simply, "Look if you wish to understand today you must read Orwell's 'Homage to Catalonia' and 'Animal Farm' followed by Huxley's 'Brave new World' anything written by Albert Camus, Whittaker Chambers 'Witness' and the works of Aleksandr Solzhenitsyn. Then you may begin to understand the enemy. Make no mistake it is an enemy. Many involved have no idea what is going on because they are what Lenin said, 'Useful idiots.'"

Waiting a moment Joseph went on, "I don't ask people to believe me, I ask people to educate themselves. Don't follow me don't listen to me, read and find the truth for yourselves."

An older doctor stepped forward, "I understand your point but we are busy we have to rely on someone to keep us abreast of events."

"I understand. The question is always simple, you can rely on the echo chamber to furnish you with the information you desire or you can go out on your own and take a stand on your own. I believe there is nothing more important than being informed. But that is your choice."

"What do you mean by echo chamber," a doctor in the back of the crowd asked.

"We live in an age of instant information. The irony is in this age we are less educated and less informed because we seek information that reinforces what we already believe. Thus we are an in an echo chamber. It is nice to hear the voices that agree with us but we have to go outside of that echo and seek knowledge on our own."

A young man stepped forward with a curious look on his face, "Mr. Buckley I read you have a doctorate from Oxford but you have argued philosophy is a sham."

Joseph paused a moment realizing the discussion was moving to a new subject. "I have always argued philosophy is nothing but an illusion. Philosophers are not looking forward they are working backward. They create a philosophy that fits that which they believe. Their philosophy doesn't change their thought process it reaffirms it. Thus philosophy is a grand deception which changes nothing as it reaffirms that which was already in existence."

Several of the listeners started to raise objections but Joseph went on ignoring them, "You each believe you are saving people as you diagnosis their illness and prescribe remedies. The question is are you or are you tools of a force beyond you? Do you save the lives of people you see or does the credit go beyond?"

A young doctor toward the front of the crowd stepped forward, "I know the answer; I save them. No one else does. There is no force beyond telling me what to do or prescribe. I save the person's life. If the person dies then is it a force beyond that killed him or her? The creator can't have it both ways. If he gets credit for saving a person he deserves the blame for killing them."

"The blame for the death of the person? Interesting view of existence. It assumes one either exists or one does not. However what if one exists beyond the world? Does existence extend beyond the earth or this it? Is the idea of a heavenly existence nothing more than a device to order society in to behaving well?"

"Are you arguing nothing we do matters?"

"I am not arguing anything, I am merely asking a question or two. In the end the answer is yours to live and die with. Let me ask one further question, if this is all there is then why do we not propose suicide as a method of relief? After all if this is it then what is the advantage in existing through pain and sorrow? What is the purpose of existence at all if one has only this life to concern one with? That is a question Albert Camus asked in his book, Myth of Sisyphus. I think he did a poor job of answering the question, but he did indeed attempt to do so."

"If one exits life one misses the good as well as the bad. One misses the opportunities life offers," a young doctor offered.

"But what advantage is there in suffering when one can simply end life. Why let a child enter the world to be raised by a Mother who is incapable of raising the child? Why place a premium on human life? We shoot horses in the head when they break a leg why not a human who is unable to walk and is confined to a wheel chair?"

"You ask questions but you don't have answers. I think you just like to stir things up. I think you are a coward afraid to take a position," an older doctor said as he pointed at Joseph.

Joseph smiled, "Perhaps I am and perhaps we all are. Or perhaps my questions confronts a truth that bothers you."

Missy made her way to the front of the group taking Joseph's arm, "Sorry but I must steal my date from you," as she pulled him toward the dance floor.

As they danced across to "Have I Told You lately," Joseph asked, "Were you afraid I was going to anger your colleagues?"

"Oh hell no. If you can get under their skin, you have my support. I just wanted to dance with you. Do you remember this song?"

Joseph paused a moment and then smiled yes, "They played it at the prom. How in the world did you arrange that?"

"Twenty dollars will arrange about anything with that band," she laughed.

As they danced he held her close looking into her eyes and then looked away afraid of what was happening. As they music came to an end she said, "Let's go, don't you think this place is a big bore?"

"Yes, but I didn't want to say that and ruin your evening."

"Let's go, I have a place I want you to see."

As Missy drove away Joseph asked, "Where are we going?"

"We are going to Cheekwood Botanical Gardens. I am going to experience everything about Christmas."

"What does it have to do with Christmas?"

"You'll see," she said as she drove up a long drive. Parking the car in a lot Joseph noticed families and couples making their way up the hill. As they approached the entrance there were green blue and red lights to the right and left.

Missy said, "This is a Christmas tradition in Nashville. They have over a million lights through the gardens with all sorts of displays. I hate to say it but I have never been here before."

As they made their way through the entrance there were reindeer in a pen with a stand selling hot chocolate. Joseph got them a hot chocolate and they began their way through the gardens of lights. There were lights along the ponds that created beautiful reflections as parents with their children stopped to spend a moment taking it all in.

As they made their way toward the mansion on the hill which once was home to the Maxwell Coffee heirs they passed through the Tunnel of lights, Candy Lane, and Trees of Light. Finally they reached the Kissing Ball where a giant mistletoe hang over head in front a large group of trees lite with bright white lights. As they walked under the mistletoe, a couple standing in the back said, "Let us take your picture."

Handing them her phone Missy stood smiling next to Joseph as he draped his arm around her. The couple yelled, "Come on you have to kiss." Looking up at the mistletoe above, Joseph leaned down and kissed Missy as they snapped the picture. The kiss continued until they heard the man laughing, "We got the picture."

As they began to walk on Joseph reached for her hand and held it as they continued through the gardens. As they toured the beautiful 30,000 square foot Georgian-style mansion they reached a room with three sets of trains running around in a room full of toys in front of a large fireplace and a Christmas tree. As the stood watching the trains and the children standing around the room looking on in awe, Missy said, "It is funny I have not thought of this in years. My favorite memory as a child was when I got a train set for Christmas. It was a Lionel with an engine three cars and a caboose. It was before my parents became so embarrassed by my weight. I wish I had that train. What about you, what was your favorite Christmas gift?"

"One Christmas my Father brought to the trailer a red Schwinn Bike. I was really excited until two days later he came to me and said he needed to get it out of town. I said no and rode it uptown and got stopped by the police. I ended up in juvenile court charged with theft. My Father never came forward and told them it was he who stole it. So, I had to see a counselor for three weeks and of course take the bike to the Morris Family and say I was sorry. That is my great Christmas memory."

"Wow, what a great memory," Missy laughed as she took Joseph's hand as they walked.

Missy drove up to Joseph's hotel and as he began to get out he said, "Great evening. I really liked the lights."

"Yes, I did too. Look tomorrow I am going to look for a tree. Do you want to go with me? You don't have to go; I realize I am taking up all of your time. So don't feel bad saying no."

Getting out of the car, Joseph looked back at Missy, "Sounds great text me the time."

As Joseph got ready for bed he opened his wallet and looked at the photo of Darcy. 'Am I being unfaithful? If I'm not why do I feel that I am? Darcy I love you. I can't go on down this road with Missy, it isn't fair to you,' he thought as he reached to turn the light off.

He tossed and turned through the night finally falling asleep as light began to shine through the window. Looking at the text he saw Missy would be there at eleven. He thought, 'I should text her back and say I can't go. I shouldn't continue down this road.' But, he didn't, he got ready and waited at the front door for her.

They found a lot with a countless number of trees and in his mind over the next thirty minutes they had examined everyone at least three times. Finally, Missy pointed to a straggly tree over to the side of the lot, "That is the tree I want."

The owner of the lot laughed, "Yeah sure lady. Really what tree do you want?"

"I am serious I want that tree."

"But lady that tree is a straggly mess. I was going to have it ground up for mulch."

"I am saving the tree. It is the one I want," Missy said with certainty.

The owner looked at Missy as if she was insane and finally said, "Hell lady you can have that tree for free and I will even throw in a stand for nothing to get rid of it."

As they drove away with the tree tied to the top of the car Joseph asked, "Why that tree?"

"It reminded me of me as a young girl. No one wanted me except you and no one could see the beauty within me except you. I looked at that tree through your eyes and I saw beauty."

As they arrived at Missy's house Joseph carried the tree into her house and sat it next to the window, as Missy requested. As they looked at the tree Joseph finally asked, "Do you have any decorations or lights?"

Missy laughed, "I didn't think about that. What are we going to do?"

Joseph looked at the tree a moment and said, "Look that tree doesn't need store bought decorations to look beautiful it needs decorations that are real and personal. Pop some popcorn and get some thread. We are making decorations."

They spent the rest of the afternoon making strings of popcorn for the tree. Missy brought some red ribbon which they used to make bows for the tree and finally Joseph saw several pine trees outside the house and ran to gather pine cones from the ground. Tying the pine cones with string they hung them on the tree.

It was late in the afternoon when they finished. The tree to most was a disaster but to them it was a beautiful work of art. Missy turned to Joseph, "Do you want to take a ride. I have a couple horses and we can ride a long distance over the neighbor's land. What do you say?"

"That sounds great."

Riding through the meadow the dark clouds began to open up with a light snow. The wind from the North hit them in the face as they rode to a small hill from where they could see the meadow. Missy's face was red from the wind and as Joseph watched her he couldn't help but think how beautiful she was. Clearly she was a beautiful woman but what made her amazing was the confidence she showed as a person. She was certain in her profession and comfortable now in her own skin. She had long left the pain of yesterday and had become a confident woman.

Missy looked at Joseph as he rode to the top of the small hill. He was comfortable in his own skin. He had taken himself from the bottom and made it to the top of his profession. An educated man confident in his beliefs as well as confident who he was. As Missy looked at him she realized they were the same person. They both had overcome the lot that was their life and made it to this point on their own. They were the same only different.

Once back they laughed and talked as they brushed down the horses finally making their way to the house and a pot of chili Missy had made. The heat of the chili warmed them and they discussed the past and present. Sitting down on the couch Missy turned on some music as they continued to talk. It was as if they couldn't find anything they didn't want to talk about, the past present and the future.

Joseph stopped and turned toward Missy, "That is Dylan."

"Yes, Don't you like Dylan."

"Oh my, I really like Dylan.

"What is your favorite Dylan song?"

Joseph thought a moment, "Forever Young."

"Wow mine too."

They sat for a moment in silence listening to Dylan, finally, Joseph said, "I guess I should call for a ride back."

"No need, just take my car. You can bring it back tomorrow."

"You want to trust your car with a former Samuels?"

Missy laughed, "I will take my chances."

"Ok, I'll bring it back tomorrow."

Taking the keys Joseph made his way out the door. Missy stood at the door watching him walk away wondering why he didn't stop to kiss her. 'I am just a fool. We are just friends, nothing more. I can't get my hopes up. I can't let him see my disappointment.'

The next morning Joseph pulled up to Missy's as she walked to the car, "Get over I am driving. I am going to take you to a place you will love."

"Where would that be?"

"Elder's Bookstore. You will love it."

Two hours after they arrived at the bookstore Joseph was still walking around in awe. He picked up a book here and there and placed them at the front desk and went back for more. He found an original copy of "Did You Ever See A Dream Walking" by Buckley as well as several Hemingways as he continued taking his finds to the front desk.

Leaving the bookstore Joseph turned to Missy, who hadn't bought anything, "That was a blast. Sorry you didn't find anything."

"I found a book. I found this," she said as she held up a book entitled 'Prodigal.'

Joseph exclaimed, "Where did you find that?"

"In the good book section," she laughed.

"That was the first book I wrote. I didn't think there was a copy out there. I am amazed you found it."

"Well I am going to have to have it autographed."

"I think you have lost your mind," Joseph laughed.

"I have a great idea. Let's have a classic movie night."

"And how are we going to do that?"

"Come on I know a place where we can get some classic movies to watch."

As they pulled into the parking lot Joseph asked, "What is this place?"

"It's McKays, they have used books and a whole lot more."

Walking in Missy made a direct shot to the classic movie section asking, "How about a Cary Grant night?"

"Sounds good to me, which ones are we getting?"

"Let me see here is North by Northwest, Arsenic and Old lace, and of course here is An Affair to Remember. What do you think?"

"Sound good to me."

CHAPTER TEN

They rode again through the meadow to the top a hill as the north cold winter wind stung their faces. Looking at Missy Joseph noticed her red cheeks and smile. In that moment he wanted to take her in his arms and never let her go, but something within held him back. Something told him to look away and say nothing that he would regret.

Finishing the ride they made their way to the house for their movie night. Missy fixed a bowl of popcorn and put North by Northwest on and settled down on the couch next to Joseph. As she took a bite of the popcorn she looked at Joseph marveling at his strong chin wavy hair and little dimples. She wanted him to reach out and grab her and hold her and never let her go. She knew she had never known anyone that made her feel the same as she felt with him. She said nothing afraid it would not be well received.

Two bowls of popcorn and three movies later Joseph said, "That was great."

"Yes, it is hard to beat Cary Grant movies."

"Well I must go it is late."

They walked to the door and as Missy looked up at him Joseph said, "I had a great time," and walked away to his car.

Walking back to the couch she slumped down wondering what was happening. 'Am I feeling something he isn't? Am I a fool chasing a dream that isn't real?'

The next day Missy kept expecting him to call but she didn't hear anything. It was the 23rd of December and she hoped he would call to make plans for Christmas. She finally left the house and rode Beauty 2 on a long ride through the meadow as the cold north wind blew small flakes of snow. Reaching the top of the hill she looked once again at her phone but there was nothing.

As she began to ride back to the house her phone rang. Stopping she quickly answered, it was him. "Missy I am sorry but I got a request to speak in Evansville tomorrow."

"A request to speak on Christmas Eve?"

"Yes the Conservative club there has a luncheon every Thursday and their speaker cancelled so they called me. I figured I would speak and then head to the airport and go home."

"Oh, so you won't be coming back?"

"I will some time but for now I should head back."

"Ok, enjoy your trip," Missy said hanging up so he wouldn't hear her cry. As the tears fell she scolded herself, 'You're a grown woman don't cry over a man.' It didn't work she continued to cry as the bitter wind hit her face.

Joseph packed his things and made his way toward Evansville and his speaking engagement. He kept telling himself, 'It is the right thing to do. I can't love again. What about Darcy?'

The room was full as Joseph got up to speak. After fifteen minutes he found his mind wandering so he quickly brought the speech to an end. As he left the stage someone asked can we ask a question or two, so he made his way back to the podium. A gentleman in the back raised his hand and asked, "Why are you running away?"

Joseph stunned quickly, "Why do you think I am running away?"

Someone close to the stage said, "No he didn't ask that, he asked, 'Is the left winning?'

Gathering himself he began an answer and in the middle said, "I am sorry but I must go. I have some business to sort."

Leaving the stage he walked to the back door and outside to his car and immediately began driving. It was if he started somewhere he would quit thinking about what he was doing. His flight was not until late from the Louisville airport so he started that way along the Ohio River on State Road 66. As he made his way he kept asking himself why was he was running, why couldn't he turn back and go to Missy. Finally as he passed the small town of Cannelton he saw a sign for a trail along the hills overlooking the Ohio River. Driving up the hill to a parking area he got out and began to walk along the trail as the bitter north winds began to blow a heavy snow in his face slowly making the path white.

Against the path limestone rocks jutted from the earth as if they were part of a fortress against the invading marauders of time bringing the future. It was clear they had lost the countless battles over the years but perhaps in the end victory would be theirs'.

Resting on a rock along the path he watched as the muddy water of the Ohio flowed toward the Mississippi River. In the distance a tiny tug boat struggled against the currents pushing four barges up the Ohio toward Louisville. As the tiny tug boat disappeared around the bend of the river another tiny tug boat pushed six barges with the current downstream toward Evansville or places unknown.

Resting there he looked at the muddy water and could not help but wonder if the next step he was to take was into the future or the past. As he pondered the next step the words he had wrote but three weeks earlier haunted him, "In the darkness of the night I looked back at the horizon and my life and saw there a desolate desert that lead to places unknown. Gathering courage I began a journey into the shifting sands that lead from whence I came to where I was going. It was in the long treacherous journey I found the lost soul that was I.”

As he sat there he pulled from his billfold a note. The note was written by Darcy just three days before she died. All this time he had carried it in his billfold but could never bring himself to read it. It was as if reading meant the end and he couldn’t face another ending. But, now as the skies filled with snow he opened the note and read her final words, “Darling you know I love you. I know you love me. And I know you have a good deal more living to do. You must move forward and love again. Please don’t do my love a disservice by not loving again. I t would break my heart thinking you refused to love again in your life. Love, Darcy. PS quit running away.”

Putting the letter back in his billfold he sat there with his tears falling as he looked through the snow at the slow moving Ohio River. He knew what he had to do. He knew what the future was for him and where it was. Making his way back to the car he began driving through the snow to the one place he knew he should be.

CHAPTER ELEVEN

Missy was getting ready to spend her evening taking down the tree since it was now a memory she didn’t want. But as she got a box out to pack things away the phone rang. It was the hospital, one of the doctors had called in sick. She thought a moment, "I might as well fill in rather than call someone else.'

So she dressed and made her way to the emergency room. The evening was uneventful with two broken arms and one drunk man and a woman who was fishing for pain killers. As the shift ended she made her way to the front desk to make sure the next crew had shown up and was ready. Mildred sitting at the desk looked up, "I thought you were going to take the time off to really enjoy Christmas?"

"Well my plan didn't work out. I guess I am not supposed to be a Christmas kind of person."

Driving home she turned down the drive to her home and noticed the lights were on. For a moment she thought about driving away but then she saw Joseph standing on the front porch. Getting out of the car she walked up to him as he smiled, "I forgot I had the key to your house."

"Oh, I see."

"No you don't see. I am a fool Missy. I was running away again and I don't want to do it anymore. You were the first person I ever loved and the person I still love. Will you forgive me for hurting you?"

"Yes, I will forgive you. I love you and I don't want to be without you. I was afraid to say it before because I didn't want to rush things but I am tired of taking it slow. I love you."

As the cold north wind blew flakes of snow around them they kissed and held as if they were afraid to let go. Finally, Joseph said I have something for you to see."

Going in the house there under the tree was a train running around the tree. "You remembered. I love it," Missy said as tears slid down her cheeks.

"Wait did you see the load the train is carrying?"

"No, what are you talking about?"

"Here on the caboose," he said as he reached down and picked something up. Slowly he bent down on a knee and said, "This ring I bought before I came to Nashville the first time to see you. I kept it and I want you to have it. But first I must ask will you marry me?"

Missy fell to her knees hugging joseph as she said, "Yes a thousand times yes."

Three months later Missy and Joseph moved into their Montana home and began in earnest their lives together. Each night they would ride out through the foothills and look in awe at the mountains that painted the skyline as they sat around a fire.

A year later Joseph stood before a group in Colorado with Missy looking on as he said, "I finally found a philosopher to follow, Jesus. I would argue He was the one true philosopher who proposed a way to live going forward not backward."